## Praise for Eric L

"As a young man, seeing that everything breaks eventually, Stuart decides to live life every day, hanging out with his friends, playing the field. Yet whenever the cicadas sing again, he must reevaluate his decision. In this engaging story of a man navigating the currents of his life, Goodman probes the way identity is formed and its fluidity."
— B. Morrison, *Innocent: Confessions of a Welfare Mother, Terrarium*

"Eric D. Goodman writes the kind of fiction a reader can love and a writer can admire."
— Jacquelyn Mitchard, first Oprah Book Club pick, *The Deep End of the Ocean*

"Supremely moving ... by turns ferocious and tender and funny from beginning to end."
— Junot Díaz, Pulitzer Prize winner, *The Brief Wonderous Life of Oscar Wao*

"Cunningly crafted."
— Madison Smartt Bell, National Book Award Nominee, *All Souls' Rising*

"Takes the craft of to the level of art. An exciting talent."
— Thomas Steinbeck, *In the Shadow of the Cypress, Down to a Soundless Sea*

"Goodman manages to capture the complicated push and pull of family, of friends, of history, of life—how it bears down on each of us, pulling us apart while simultaneously pushing us together. His characters are, in turn, compassionate, indifferent, bitter, sympathetic, wistful, and most of all, real."
— Mary Beth Keane, *Ask Again Yes, The Walking People*

"Tight, taut, terrific."
— Steve Berry, *The Templar Legacy, The Amber Room*

"Sincere and empathetic, brims with soulful compassion."
— Victoria Patterson, *Drift, This Vacant Paradise*

"Warm, poignant, funny, and suspenseful."
— Lucrecia Guerrero, *Tree of Sighs, Chasing Shadows*

"An absolute delight... beautifully written... will hypnotically pull you in and captivate you to the very end."
— Jessica Anya Blau, *Drinking Closer to Home, Summer of Naked Swim Parties*

"By turns comic and poignant. Engagingly original"
— Yona Zeldis McDonough, *In Dahlia's Wake, The Four Temperaments*

"Utterly unique. Humorous, thoughtful, unexpected."
— Jennifer Miller, *The Heart You Carry Home, Year of the Gadfly*

"Strange and wonderful."
— Michael Kimball, *Us, Big Ray, Dear Everybody*

"There is real suspense in this brave book."
— Ron Tanner, *Missile Paradise*

"A tenderhearted story that's laced with grace."
— Jen Grow, *My Life as a Mermaid*

"One of Baltimore's most riveting and prolific writers."
— Katherine Cottle, *The Hidden Heart of Charm City*

"A good read under the Big Top of a fine craftman's imagination."
— Rafael Alvarez, *The Wire, The Fountain of Highlandtown*

"Clever, witty, captivating!"
— Toby Devens, *Barefoot Beach, Happy Any Day Now*

"A tight, breathtaking tapestry."
— Bathsheba Monk, *Now You See It ... Stories from Cokesville, PA*

"Goodman isn't letting you move until you've turned all these nimble pages."
—Jerry Holt, *The Killing of Strangers*

"A gripping read. Will stay in my mind for years to come."
— Tom Glenn, *Last of the Annamese*

"Goodman's mastery of the language makes this a treat you'll want to savor."
— Austin S. Camacho, *Blood and Bone, Collateral Damage*

"An unforgettable journey that cuts deep."
— Patry Francis, *The Liar's Diary, All the Children are Home*

"A riveting page-turner."
— *Baltimore Review*

"Goodman is a born storyteller."
— *New York Journal of Books*

"Irresistible."
— *The Writer Magazine*

# WRECKS AND RUINS

# WRECKS AND RUINS

Eric D. Goodman

Apprentice House Press
Loyola University Maryland

First Edition

Casebound ISBN: 978-1-62720-383-8
Paperback ISBN: 978-1-62720-384-5
Ebook ISBN: 978-1-62720-385-2

Printed in the United States of America

Design by Dan Darlak
Edited by Alondra Vargas Posada
Promotion plan by Ava Therien

Cover art: cicada sketch from the archives of the Smithsonian's National Museum of Natural History; wood photograph by Patrick Fore

Internal art by Vincent van Gogh

Published by Apprentice House Press

Apprentice
House Press
*Loyola University Maryland*

Apprentice House Press
Loyola University Maryland
4501 N. Charles Street
Baltimore, MD 21210
410.617.5265
www.ApprenticeHouse.com
info@ApprenticeHouse.com

*For Cliff, Dave, Steve, and Jeff*

# Contents

*Wrecks and Ruins* finds its beginnings in the short story "Cicadas," which took place in 2004.

"Cicadas" was originally published in New Lines from the Old Line State: An Anthology of Maryland Writers in 2008.

An abridged version of "Cicadas" was featured on Baltimore's National Public Radio (NPR) station, 88.9 FM, WYPR later that same year.

*"Some things are more precious because they don't last long."*
— *Oscar Wilde*

*"The world breaks everyone, and afterword,*
*some are strong at the broken places."*
—*Ernest Hemingway*

# HOW A COLLECTION BEGINS

Sometimes, things that normally do not belong together, when forced into close proximity, result in collaborations of unique beauty. Like the shuffling of notes into a song that makes the light hairs on an attentive listener's arm stand on end. Like the meeting of heat, fuel, and oxygen in a wooden rowhouse that bursts into glorious flame and lights an otherwise lightless night. The rolling of words into lines that form a poem to send chills up and down a reader's spine. Or two vehicles at a faulty-lighted intersection colliding, twisting together into one metallic sculpture worthy of display in a museum of modern art. The freeze-thaw frost wedging and erosion over millions of years that result in majestic rock formations such as the hoodoos of Bryce Canyon. Or, like the joining of two broken people who discover that they are better as a couple than as individual loners.

Cicada husks, ticket stubs, hood ornaments, elongated coins, crushed toys, shattered dishes, photographs, and memories—these were the fragments that filled out Stuart's jagged life as an adult.

When Stu was five years old, he and his father crossed over the railroad tracks one afternoon. Dad took a penny from his pocket, placed it on the iron rail, and stepped aside. The locomotive's massive power mesmerized Stu. The solid penny had flattened into an oblong swath of copper, Abe Lincoln's elongated profile barely visible. As Stu grew older, the keepsake on his dresser reminded him that some items held more weight—more meaning—when distressed or damaged.

At six, Stu and his friends played on the sidewalks and in the dirt with their Matchbox Cars and Hot Wheels. Some of his friends liked to keep their miniature show cars clean; others preferred the mud-speckled, off-road look. Stu found that he preferred more than just a little mud on his cars. While some kids were racing and cleaning their wheels, Stu would set his cars on death-defying missions, dragging them through muddy puddles, scraping them across corrugated metal, rolling them through wet paint, crushing them between large rocks. During a visit to his grandparents, his toy cars had many obstacles along the gravel driveway—stones denting the roof and doors and damaging the tires. Grandma and Grandpa expressed their concern to his parents: "Better keep an eye on him. What if he's inclined to inflict damage on real vehicles when he became old enough to drive?"

When Stu was seven, Mom got Stu and Dad a train set. They assembled the tracks on a wooden table in the basement, set up the miniature community, and put the little train in motion. Stu brought the locomotive carefully around the bends, through the dark tunnels, slowing it to a halt at the first sign of trouble. In time, it took more than a smooth ride to satisfy him. One day, two pieces of track were askew. Stu engineered the train forward at full speed until it hit the uneven tracks. The train derailed, slid across the table, and tumbled over the edge, crashing to the basement's cement floor. Stu placed the broken engine on his bedroom dresser, next to his flattened penny, pet rock, rabbit's foot, and his favorite crushed Matchbox Car.

As a teen, Stu returned to the full-size railroad tracks in his neighborhood, not to flatten pennies, but to look for ruins. Bottle caps, rusty rail spikes, suitcase handles, rusted horseshoes, oddly shaped chunks of metal, scraps thrown from train windows and caught between the wheels and the tracks. He found a broken pocket watch, the tattered remains of a leather-bound daily planner, a bent wedding ring, even the twisted-off hood ornament of a Buick. These items were meaningful to Stu because they had histories. Their extreme experiences had infused them with character.

In those turbulent teenaged years, Stu began to see that these histories—these extreme experiences—were not unlike the experiences that created character in people. Or that damaged them. He watched helplessly as his parents argued over the stupidest things—who had the most car accidents or got the most speeding tickets, who spent the most money on unnecessary luxuries or spent the least time saying they were sorry. Stu wasn't sure whether this was all new, part of their decaying marriage, or whether they had always fought like this and he was just becoming mature enough to know what it meant.

Most of the parental arguments were loud, but only verbal. Occasionally a towel or glass or plate might get thrown. One autumn afternoon, after Mom and Dad stormed off in opposite directions at the heated conclusion of a fight, leaving a splintered Wedgewood platter on the kitchen floor, Stu took the initiative to clean up the mess. He kept the largest shard of the plate and added it to his collection. Two birds hovered, face to face, in the blue pattern. Feeling that, perhaps, some items in his collection were too personal to place on display, Stu stowed the platter shard in a small cardboard box under his bed.

The quiet experiences of degeneration Stu witnessed were even more troubling than the loud ones. As Stu visited the homes of his childhood friends, Clint, Skip, and Dana, he sensed what was seen but not said, or said but not meant.

Clint's dad loved football more than family and devoted more time to his television set than anything else. The wooden console sat like a shrine on the rusty shag carpet of their living room, a long and narrow yarn afghan on top of the great wooden cube, cradling a few knick-knacks and a framed family portrait. Nobody seemed to look at the things on top of the set except for Stu—everyone else focused on the screen, normally tuned into a sporting event or game show.

Stu's other friend, Skip, spent a lot of time watching television with his parents. Skip's family watched their television set together—usually shows about family values and love between neighbors who never knocked, laugh tracks always swooping in to save viewers from being overcome by any genuine emotion—but Skip's family couldn't be more apart. At least Clint's parents passively griped about one another from time to time. Skip's parents only spoke out of necessity. **Time for dinner. Time for Wheel of Fortune. Time for grown-up programming. Time for Stu to go home.**

And then there was Stu's friend Dana. It was always loud at Dana's house because his mom and dad were always yelling at each other. "Woman, where's my glasses?" "Boy, you better keep track of your own glasses and stop hounding me." Part of the reason they had to yell was to hear each other over the music—they nearly always had a CD or vinyl record or cassette tape playing in the background. They barely ever had the television on, but there was always background music at Dana's house. And what sounded like vicious fighting at first soon came to sound to Stu like another language for love. "Get your ass over here and give me some sugar." "Don't make me take my belt off!" Not at all like the bickering between Stu's own parents.

Stu wondered why nobody's parents got along normally, why none of them could talk to one another the way he and his friends talked to each other—maturely, respectfully, like adults. None of their parents seemed anything like the ones on television or even like the ones in the love songs.

Stu preferred the out-loud, on-the-table fighting in his own home to the reverberating tension at Clint's house, or the mundane complacency at Skip's, or even the funny faux fighting at Dana's. Stu preferred the open unrest at home, even when that hostility ended in a temporary separation and finalized itself in a divorce.

Seeing the romantic relationships in his adult role models fail did not stop Stu from wanting to start one of his own. At a time when he was teetering between childhood and adulthood, in 1987, the seventeen-year cicadas hummed excitedly all around them. It was like background music to the excitement humming within him when he spent time around Skye.

Angelic and graceful, Skye was a front-row fixture in his elective World Lit class, drawing him out from the back row and into the second. He elected to take the course not because he was interested in literature, but because he had heard that

Skye—the senior he'd seen in the lunchroom and on the school grounds—was enrolled. This was a rare opportunity to join her in a mixed-grade course, to provide an excuse for him to talk to her without sounding like a creep, or worse, like a loser.

While the teacher droned on about poetry and literature and the difference between metaphors and similes, Stu focused on the visible part of Skye's neck when her soft, blonde hair was up, or at her lower legs when she wore a sundress. In the halls, and then outside, Stu courted Skye alongside the cicadas, serenaded her with their voices instead of his own, and, later, loved her alongside them during camping trips and romantic getaways. Before the cicada's eggs were falling from tree branches and delivering offspring to burrow into the earth for another seventeen years, Stu's and Skye's relationship was beginning to dry up. Soon, it would be crushed like the insect husks covering the sidewalks.

Stu harbored hope that his love with Skye could last for at least a little longer. Why say farewell to a summer love when the opportunity of a fall fling waited on the cicada-cloaked horizon? She was two years older than he was, and Stu appreciated her maturity and experience. Despite his casual beginning with her, he found he wanted to keep his arms around Skye for as long as he could hold her.

"Want to take a road trip?" Stu had asked her as they sat on a park bench on a sunny day. He tried to hold her hands in his, but she kept pulling them away.

"I'll be going off to college in another month," she said. It wasn't a surprise; it wasn't something she hadn't mentioned before. It just had never seemed that important to Stu since it was weeks away and he knew they were only a temporary thing.

That temporary thing had grown on him, time had grown short, and Stu wanted to make their relationship more permanent. "Maybe I can convince you to stay here." Stu pulled her closer to him and kissed her.

She gave in to the kiss, but did not give in to his bigger picture. "I don't see us as something that's going to last forever," she said.

Stu's smile dropped. "Nothing lasts forever."

"That's right," Skye said. "Not even marriage. Not that you're the marrying type."

"Marriage is just a sham, anyway," Stu said defensively. "A piece of paper designed to hold people together even after they've grown apart. The Beatles didn't sing *All you need is a marriage certificate.*"

On that late summer afternoon, Skye's cautious smile was more troubling than titillating. "So, let's just enjoy what we have now, while it lasts. Here and now." She kissed him, and the disconcerting mood lifted.

That's how it always was when uncomfortable subjects threatened to pry Skye and Stu apart. All it took was a kiss, a touch, or an embrace from Skye to push discomfort aside. They had the tools it took to make it easy to focus on the pleasure of the moment.

As summer began to fade, the cicadas left behind thousands of husks, baked onto the trees and along the sidewalks. The insects had enjoyed their moment in the sun, and this was the result of their short-lived excitement. Stu collected a plastic bag full of husks and strung them together into a necklace for Skye.

"Each one of these little guys lived and loved," Stu said in an attempt to readjust her confused expression. "They burned out instead of fading away."

Skye forced a smile as she reluctantly put it on, seeming to check it with her eyes and her fingertips every few moments to make sure none of them were crawling on her neck or burrowing beneath her blouse.

"It's the most, uh, unique gift I've ever received."

Stu discerned she was finding a way toward truth without stating that she'd rather have received something more traditional to wrap around her neck.

"I thought you deserved a gift with some thought and creativity behind it, not just some factory-produced necklace from the mall."

Skye nodded. Stu kissed her, and she melted back into her usual self.

It wasn't long after that afternoon—just a week or so later—that Skye decided to break up with Stu, giving him back the necklace. The cicada necklace was a keepsake; it reminded him of buzzing, excitement, and his short-lived romance with the first girl he loved. He added the necklace to the collection crowding his bedroom dresser. Every time he looked at the cicada necklace, he understood that burning out wasn't really all that much better than fading away after all. He decided it was better fit for the cardboard box beneath his bed, beneath the place where he'd once held Skye.

For his last two years of high school, Stu continued to date women—but decided not to get too close. He confided in his friends, Clint, Skip, and Dana, as they played cards, hung out at diners, and went on hikes. He held girls physically close, but emotionally at an arm's length.

Clint, already sporting a full black beard in their junior year that seemed to contradict his high school letterman jacket, gave his advice. "Don't play the field, Stu. Once you find a cutie you like, latch on to her. I'm not doing anything to screw up my thing with Amanda."

Dana disagreed. "Listen to this fool." Dreadlocks swayed as he shook his head at Clint, then spoke directly to Stu. "Man, just because you dig hamburgers don't mean you've got to eat hamburger every day. Keep exploring that menu. The next course might be the best."

Skip's shrug was barely visible beneath his long red hair. "I don't know how you guys do it. No one ever offers me a menu. Not that I need one; I'd be happy with what Clint's got going on."

"Like I said," Clint reiterated, "you guys can try to open your Baskin-Robbins. I picked my flavor."

When Clint got his girlfriend pregnant and dropped out of high school to marry her, Stu was beside himself and could finally understand why a person might want to throw a Wedgewood platter at someone. "How could you ruin your life like this?" Stu asked Clint. "Over a girl?"

"Maybe Amanda's the best thing to ever happen to him," Skip had defended. "I'd trade places with him in a heartbeat."

"Don't you guys realize we're too young for a life sentence?" Stu ranted. He poked Clint in the chest. "You're throwing your life away."

When Stu wasn't on a date or hanging out with his friends, he sometimes sat in his room with headphones on, listening to compact disks. Music was a pastime he continued to embrace, even as he moved away and grew older. Music was a friend he could count on day in and day out, even when his school buddies were miles away. There were so many musical discoveries—both old and new—and the reliable favorites never changed on him. The songs were always there, unfailing, and there was never a need to try to impress them. He could just let go and listen.

When Clint dropped out of high school—just four months shy of graduating—Stu was going through a Rolling Stones stage. Years later, in 2003, when Skip finally found a girl who loved him and he asked Stu to be his best man, Stu found himself searching for the song that had spoken to him back when Clint tied the knot. The song had more meaning to it, Stu being older and having more fully lived the lyrics. Stu felt that all his friends from school had grown up and settled down. They had all "mortgaged their lives."

Stu sometimes felt as though he was sitting on a fence, and that his friends only got married because they had nothing else to do. He had better things to do with his life.

# LAS VEGAS, NEVADA

## WINTER 2020

# MOMENTARY LAPSE OF CERTAINTY

Stuart found it hard to believe that he was finally going to do it. *They* were going to do it. So much time together had made their decision seem a natural one. They had been so different, but fit together so well together, like lawyers on opposite sides of a court case who went out for dinner and drinks on a regular basis. Stuart and Tiffany did have things in common, but they had far more in opposition. They were so unalike, they looked and acted like politicians slinging tweets at one another long after most people had gone to sleep.

The truth was, Stuart realized as he reminisced over their years together, most of those tweets were little love letters. Yet, Stuart reassured himself during yet another momentary lapse of certainty, love was, after all, as natural or unnatural as anything else in life: celebrations, disasters, creations, wrecks, fortresses, ruins.

Sitting in their split-level luxury suite in The Venetian along with his closest friends, Stu realized they were half-wrecked already. The night was old, well past midnight, but their celebration was still wet behind the ears. And yet, not quite wet enough.

Clint hovered over Stuart. "Here, Stu, have another!" The mixed drink—bourbon and Coke on the rocks—caused the old-fashion glass to sweat. Slouching in his high-back leather throne in the center of the lower half of their suite, a living room with a wall of windows looking over the Vegas strip, Stu accepted the beverage. Stu spent a moment looking at the etched crystal glass, then up at Clint, and back at the chilled drink. Clint, who was twice Stu's size, looked like a boss in his dark blue pinstripe suit, white shirt, and red tie. He was shorter than Stu by half a foot, but made up for it in heft and aggressiveness. "Drink up," he insisted. Droplets of bourbon clung to the gray and brown hairs of his full beard. "We're supposed to get you drunker than a skunk tonight."

Skip, who lounged passively on a loveseat to the left, nursed another Southern Comfort straight up. "He looks like he's enjoying himself, Clint. Why don't you just let him drink at his own pace?"

Clint swiveled away from Stu and made his way toward Skip, a bull just itching for a red flag to charge. "Oh, that's great, coming from Mr. I-want-one-glass-of-water-with-every-drink." He waved his hand dismissively at Skip and Stu. "You guys are lightweights."

Skip sat up, placing his boats on the carpeted floor. He sported a pullover Polo shirt and jeans. He had abandoned his long hair long ago and now wore his copper and silver hair in a traditional business cut. Skip raised his glass with a grin and took another drink. "It's called hydration, my friend."

Clint grunted. "This is supposed to be a bachelor party! Drink up, men!"

Dana, now a professional DJ and the high school friend who had performed at each of their wedding receptions, hunched over his laptop and dropped the metaphorical needle on another tune. It was a top-40 hip-hop hit that Stu recognized from the radio but didn't really know. Dana stood up and strutted toward them, finding his seat in a bright orange high back next to Skip's loveseat. He smiled contently as he took a Hennessey from the glass side table and raised it to the others. "To each his own. We're all feeling good tonight, fellas, no matter what we drink." Even inside their suite, Dana wore his purple, felt, wide-brimmed hat. It matched his suede jacket and worked well with his yellow button-down. He almost looked like he should be carrying a cane.

Given their current state, the music sounded good, even if it wasn't really Stu's usual musical scene. Stu nodded to the beat as he scanned the room, a smile completing his expression as his eyes completed their rotation. Skip and Dana on one side, Clint now back to his sofa on the other, a well-stocked bar on the side table, and in front of them, like a big-screen television, glowed the large window overlooking the Vegas strip below with an incredible view of the Bellagio Fountain. This was the console TV set of their generation—one that you could jump into at any moment or simply sit back and enjoy. This was comfort with a twist of elation.

The four men—now in their early 50s—had gone to high school together in Virginia. After graduation, they had gone their separate ways, but managed to get together two or three times a year for their little stag getaways. Sometimes it was a party in Vegas. Other times, a backpacking trip in Utah's Sawtooth Mountains or Wyoming's Teton range. Sometimes a cabin in the woods; other times, a party in the city. Stu had learned over the past thirty-plus years that he could depend on these guys to be there. If they weren't interested in talking about serious issues, at least they could be counted on to drink and play cards and chit-chat. They could be counted on to just be there, which was oftentimes enough. Talking about serious issues often happened between them, usually taking the disguise of being a by-product of seemingly less meaningful activities.

For each of them, this was their first getaway since the COVID-19 pandemic imprisoned them each in their own home. They were all working remotely now and had all been tested prior to being allowed to fly. They knew they were clear, safe—but couldn't be so sure about the still-existent crowds in the strip below. In their current state, they weren't that worried about it.

Dana hadn't simply selected a song—this was a week-end-long playlist. The wireless speakers went from one song to another. With half-full glasses, everyone sat and relaxed. Stu stood, drawn by the television-esque wall. He slowly walked toward the bright-light view outside. The fountain danced, almost as if to the music Dana had selected. The fountain was beautiful, but the Bellagio had another feature that Stu loved even more: the elaborate ceiling of colorful art glass in its lobby. Earlier in the night, between drinking and gambling, they had passed through the Bellagio lobby and Stu had been transfixed by the jellyfish-like shapes of many colors hovering above them. It was a beautiful mess, perfect in its imperfection. He fantasized about taking a small, heavy object from his pocket—perhaps a worry stone or key fob or hood ornament—and throwing it at the ceiling while no one was paying attention. How amazing that rain of rainbow-colored art glass would be. The photographs he could take of such an event with the right camera and film. The freshly broken shards of rainbow on the ground, just waiting to be claimed.

"Hey, Stu, what's on your mind?" Skip had left his loveseat and now stood beside him.

Stu woke from his fantasy, refocused his view, staring at the window, and saw his reflection next to Skip's— it surprised him to see two middle-aged men looking back at him. For most of the past twenty years he had worn a stubbly black beard to make himself look older. Recently, he had shaven his gray beard off to make himself look younger. Stu admired his own comfortable stonewashed silk button-down shirt of gray and knit blue slacks. Stu adjusted his focus and looked again at the scenery below them. He put an arm around Skip and pointed with his almost-empty glass to the lit-up strip below: flashing signs and casino entrances, cruising cars and mobs of people. "All of that …" Clint and Dana had gotten up to look at the scene below them. "All of that is waiting for us."

Clint laughed, walking to the bar to pour himself another drink. "It won't wait forever, gentlemen. Refill your drinks and let's jump in.

# BOSS WALK

Stu, Clint, Skip, and Dana left their suite in the Venetian and began walking leisurely down the hall. Dana surprised them with what he had in his little shoulder sling: music boomed from it, as loud as it had been in their room. Like theme music, the low bass pounded out their steps down the hotel hallway, into the elevator, through the lobby, by the indoor street scenes of Venice and gondolas cruising along indoor canals. The men had filled their crystal old-fashions and carried their drinks with them.

"Look at those losers," Clint said, pointing at the couples seated at what looked like an outdoor square café that was indoors. "Middle-aged morons."

"Don't forget," Skip said. "We're middle-aged morons now."

Stu scoffed. "If we're lucky. None of us are gonna live to be 100."

Dana took a gulp of his Hennessey on ice. "Speak for yourself. You're only as old as you feel. And I'm feeling pretty young tonight."

They practically yelled at one another as they conversed; it was the only way to be heard over the blaring music coming from the portable speaker in Dana's sling bag. Stu remembered visits to Dana's house, his parents yelling over the sound of music. In the Venetian's street-café scene, people looked at the four men, disturbed by the music and loud yelling and hotel barware in hand. Knowing that eyes were on them, they put an extra swagger in their steps; they weren't walking—they *strutted* out the front doors of The Venetian and onto the strip.

Stu, Clint, Skip, and Dana bulldozed through the crowd at their own pace, creating a little bubble around their four bodies with music, conversation, and a laid-back vibe. The Coronavirus that had cooped up the nation for the better part of 2020 was still present, but it didn't calm the Vegas strip during relaxed restrictions. Frat boys and sorority girls passed by in t-shirts and tight skirts; business men walked by in suits and Dockers; ladies strolled along in ball gowns and short skirts; clans of mothers out for a night away from the family howled at the moon in mom jeans casual wear. Some people wore medical masks, fashionable cloth masks, or plastic face shields. Others didn't bother, emboldened by alcohol, sure what was in their system would kill anything that tried to enter it.

On the street, cars and limos and trucks with dancing girls on poles in back cruised stop-and-go as the traffic and traffic lights kept them idling at a slower pace than the people on the sidewalks. Drug deals went down on some corners and negotiations between men and scantily clad women on other corners. Two women brushed against Dana and Clint as they passed by and then giggled as they exchanged looks.

Dana sighed. "Ah, Vegas."

Skip spoke under his breath. "I don't think that was six feet apart, guys."

Dana fixed Skip with a dismissive glance. "Man, the rules don't apply here. Anything goes."

Clint chuckled. "Boys, the playground doesn't get much bigger than this."

Stu nodded, then said, "There's always Dubai. It's supposed to be like Vegas on steroids."

Skip put a hand on Stu's arm. "Dude, look around. I think this place is already on steroids."

Clint finished off his drink and tossed the hotel barware in the bushes. "I'm gonna take my brush with that lovely lady as a sign of luck. Let's gamble."

Skip nodded his head. "Haven't you already lost enough, Clint?"

"Hey, I'm ahead. Sure, I lost a few hundred at poker. But not until I won twice that at roulette."

"So you're only half a loser," Stu said.

Clint gave Stu a buddy punch. "Let's see who loses now."

Temporarily stalled by the explosions from the pirate show in front of Treasure Island, they entered the casino and found an empty blackjack table. The four of them took their seats. "Hey, darling," Clint said to the dealer.

"Oh boy," Skip put his forehead on his open hand.

"Good evening, gentlemen." The dealer wore a sequenced mask, but you could see her inviting smile in the structure of her eyes.

"Mind if we have a conversation while we play?" Clint asked her. "Since we own the table?"

"Not at all," the dealer said. "As long as you don't mind turning off that music while you're in here."

"Yes ma'am," Dana said. He took out his phone and paused the music.

The tall, black blackjack dealer dealt their cards. Skip was the first to yell, "Hit me."

"Hey," Clint called out to a passing cocktail waitress. "What do we got to do to get some drinks around here?"

Stu put an arm on Clint's shoulder. "Calm down, man."

Dana grinned. "Papa's thirsty. Let him have his drink."

Skip fake-squinted at Clint as though bringing him into focus. "You are starting to look like Papa Hemingway a bit."

Clint frowned. "I'll take my touch of gray to your glint of red any day."

Dana laughed. "*Touch* of gray? I think you've dipped in more than a toe, my friend."

"Maybe I need a clown hat to hide it."

Dana pinched the brim of his hat. "This baby's more Prince than Joker."

"You used to have style," Clint shot back with a laugh. "Now you're *The Artist Formerly Known as Fashionable*."

By the end of their first hands—Clint was down, Dana was up—their drinks arrived. "Kind of watery," Clint said, staring at the glass. "We were mixing much better drinks in our suite."

"Yeah, but the action's out here," Dana said. Behind the beautiful blackjack dealer, on a catwalk, women had begun dancing in barely-there sequined coverings. "Hit me, darling."

They drank another round and continued playing black-jack, flirting with the dealer, ogling the dancers, and talking.

"Hey," Clint said playfully to the dealer. "Why don't you take that thing off so we can see how pretty you are?"

The dealer coolly dealt another hand. "We're not allowed to remove our masks while we're dealing. Casino policy."

Clint's raised eyebrow was nearly comical. "Who said anything about your mask?"

If the words irritated her, she tsked it off without showing it.

Shrugging it off, Clint said, "Well, if you won't hit on me, then just hit me."

She did, and the sum of his cards came to 23. "Oh!" Clint grunted and spun around in his stool.

"Out and out," Dana dissed.

"All part of my strategy," Clint came back.

Playing cards was something they'd done since high school, although it had not been nearly as glamorous in the school cafeteria. It seemed that every time they got together, at one point or another they ended up playing cards. Stu had realized at one point, years ago, that the cards were a comfortable excuse for having deeper conversation. Especially when they were younger, it felt weird to approach one another with "I need to talk to you about something personal." But in the playing of cards, any conversation could be planted. They pretended that the card game was the focus and that the conversation was a by-product. But in reality, they'd all come to understand that cards had been a cover for allowing them to share their feelings.

Their cafeteria card games had begun in the second year of high school and carried them to graduation. As soon as their rectangular pizza slices and chocolate milks had been consumed, they would put aside their plastic trays and take out their plastic-filmed paying cards. Their usual games had been spades, hearts, and 7-up. Once they left school, they tried poker and pinochle. At the moment, it was blackjack.

"Hit me," Stu said, then folded.

Clint said, "Can you believe it? We're playing cards. Just like back in the day."

"We always do," Skip said in a sing-song voice indicating that this was a comfort subject. "It's like a way of life. The way of the card."

Clint laughed. "I'll bet way back when we were spades in high school, you never expected that in the year 2020, we'd be playing cards like this!" He motioned his hand to the flashing lights and bells and chimes, their beautiful dealer, and the attractive dancers gyrating just beyond her.

Dana surrendered his hand. "You may be experienced card players, but this deck is stacked against us. We were having better luck at roulette."

"Good point," Stu said. They finished their drinks, tipped their dealer, and headed back out to the strip.

# RENDER UNTO CAESAR

Back outside in the lit-up night, they resumed their strut down the strip with music booming from Dana's shoulder bag. Two masked couples walked in a straight line past them, appearing uncomfortable to be here in the crowd, causing Stu to wonder why they would come to Vegas in the first place. A group of poorly singing thirty-somethings passed by and nearly drowned out their loud music. The men and women staggered with giant, plastic tumblers hanging from straps around their necks, heavy with red sludge. Seeing the sad sight pass them by made them realize they were dry. They felt strangely incomplete.

Clint pulled a silver flask from the breast pocket of his pinstripe jacket and passed it around. "Maker's Mark hits the mark."

Skip looked worried when Stu passed the flask to him. "Should we be drinking out of the same container?

"We're all clear, we know that. We're part of the same bubble."

That convinced Skip, and he took a swig and passed it to Dana.

An amber streak ran down Clint's beard.

"Hits the spot," Dana said, pointing. "Looks like part of it hits your beard, too."

Skip winced. "We should probably put some food in our stomachs while there's still room."

"We already ate dinner," Stu said.

"Dude," Skip groaned, "that was eight hours ago."

Dana looked at his silver and gold watch. "Skip's right. It's already 3 a.m."

Clint grunted. "The night's young."

"No," Skip corrected. "The morning's young. The night's done gone."

Stu pointed to a White Castle in the distance. "I never thought I'd want to wait in a long line for those little bites. But they sure sound good now."

"Let's get a sack," Clint agreed.

As they waited in line, they watched as face-masked workers sprayed and wiped down all of the surfaces between customers departing and new ones sitting down. A muffled cashier operator took their order and another masked worker had their order sacked up before the credit card transmission made it through.

The four of them sat on bar stools at a tall table in the center of the open-door restaurant, two sacks of little, square hamburgers between them, a soda for each of them plus a cup of water for Skip, determined to remain hydrated.

"Hydrate with this," Clint said as he poured the remains of his flask into their sodas.

Dana lifted his wax-coated paper cup. "To the next menu item on your table, Stu. May it be the best course of your life."

Skip lifted his cup. "I never thought we'd be celebrating this."

Clint lifted his own waxy cup, hamburger grease already streaking the cup's blue logo. "That's right. Here's to a guy who knows how to have his cake and eat it too!"

Stu hit cups with the others, a moshing sound in place of the usual clinking. "You guys are too much. Thanks for indulging me."

They all drank, then shoved steamed buns and meat into their mouths.

Dana chuckled. "It'll be an unusual ceremony. I'm not sure what to put on the playlist."

"Party music!" Stu laughed. "It'll be a celebration!"

"More like a prison sentence," Skip said. "Or exile from life as you know it."

Clint licked his fingers after his last bite. "You're dwelling on later, but now is now. Let's celebrate now!"

Skip gulped down the last of his water, and the four men carried their paper-cup bourbon colas back onto the strip. Dana pressed a button and their bubble of music resumed.

Clint pointed to a sign in the distance. "Caesar's Palace?"

Skip put his hand up for a high five. "Let's do it!" The others left him hanging as they proceeded toward another casino.

At Cesar's Palace, they didn't wait for a cocktail waitress to bring them the free watered-down drinks; they went to the bar and ordered tall cocktails in high-ball glasses. Stu didn't even know what they were drinking—Dana had ordered the drinks and passed them out—but the cocktails were sweet and sour and orange-red. They tasted as smooth and mellow as Stu felt.

"Let's hit the roulette table," Clint said.

"I'm down with that," Dana agreed. Stu and Skip merrily followed along.

They'd begun their party around noon, nearly 17 years ago. *Hours ago*, Stu corrected himself. It's not like they were stringing cicada cycles together with their parties. They'd started the celebration up in their split-level luxury suite at The Venetian, where they had three bedrooms and a sleeper sofa in the living room, a stocked bar, and a marvelous view of the strip. Then they'd gone down to gamble—roulette, slots, poker, blackjack—before dinner at a Japanese restaurant with a giant Buddha towering over two open floors of dining space. After raw beef strips served with a hot stone for self-cooking, they'd returned to drinking and gambling in the casinos, trying just about everything except craps—that was too complicated for their altered states. They jumped on the indoor-outdoor roller coaster, petted the MGM lion's paw, stared at the light beam from the top of the Luxor pyramid that supposedly shot out farther into space than any other light from earth, and visited New York and Paris in the same hour. Then, around eight, they decided to take a "break" and juice up in their suite, where they sat for a couple of hours and drank proper cocktails while listening to music and talking about their lives: Clint and his rocky relationship with Amanda; Skip and his conveyer-belt comfort with Leona; Dana and the two girls he was currently dating; and the woman Stu loved, Tiffany. Then, it was back to the larger party on the strip, hotel old-fashions with clinking ice in hand, and a cloud of music pulsating from Dana's bagged wireless speaker enveloping them.

"I have a system that I think works over time," Skip said as he placed his bets at the roulette wheel.

Dana laughed. "You and every other fool who blows their paycheck. Just one more spin to win!"

Stu shook his head at both of them. "You just have to allot yourself a spefisic amount of money to blow, then have fun with it."

"Spefisic?" Dana laughed again. "Or specific?"

"It's only money," Clint said as he tossed some chips on the table. "Made to spend." That's the kind of attitude Stu had come to expect from Clint, who at one time had worked three jobs simultaneously to get one of his three kids through college. His second child had gone to community college for two years and the third had decided against higher education for the opportunity to get higher more often. All three of them had moved out and must have been in their late 20s and early 30s by now. It was when Stu thought about details like this that he remembered how damn old they were now. Just yesterday it seemed that he and Clint, Skip and Dana were the thirty-somethings. Not Clint's kids. Stu shook his head and refocused on the spinning roulette wheel.

As the perky roulette spinner flirted with the four of them, as the cocktail waitress brought them drinks—weaker, healthier, more hydrating—they collectively won more at the roulette table than they lost.

Dawn was arriving outside, but here in Caesar's Palace, one would never have a way of knowing it—at least, not without the aid of a timepiece smuggled in from the outside, like a watch or smartphone. It was late-night party time 24 hours a day in the windowless Vegas interiors—lights flashing, bells ringing, smokers filling the air with stale swirls of smoke that formed their own personal rainclouds. It may have been inching toward workday for people in other parts of the land, but here in Vegas—in Caesar's Palace—it was the middle of the night and the center of the party.

The girls still prowling the blackjack and crap tables, poker and roulette wheels at this hour were aware of the time, and had lowered their sights as night gave way to day. The high rollers in the semi-private areas of the casino were emptying, outnumbered by the chain smokers with oxygen tanks seated at the penny and nickel slots who were ever more productive these days since they only needed to push their buttons over and over and could ignore the labor of the levers to their lefts.

Stu, Clint, Skip, and Dana thought they were hot stuff, their confidence having ballooned throughout the course of the evening with increasing alcohol, music, strutting, and just enough winning to keep them playing. Later, on their rides home, they would realize that the early-morning ladies were settling, but in the moment, as they sat around the spinning roulette wheel, they knew they were winners and that the women standing behind them wanted to be a part of their entourage. With sultry glances and hoarse giggles, four ladies joined the four men at the table, sitting alongside them, placing no bets of their own on the table but hedging their bets for some profit just the same.

Dana called the cocktail waitress over. "These beauties look thirsty."

Clint scoffed. "Yeah! Money's no object. Get these ladies the best free drinks you've got!"

The women laughed. Stu realized they must hear stuff like this all the time, jokes and one-liners as stale as the cigarette smoke surrounding them.

"Man," Skip said under his breath but still loud for everyone around to hear. "Why didn't we come here *before* I was married?"

Dana clicked his tongue. "Ain't nothing but a thing, man."

Clint said, "Hey, we're in Vegas, Skip. What happens here stays here."

"I'm single," Dana said. "I don't care if it stays here or not."

"You got that right," Stu said. "Let it follow me if it wants to."

# WRECKED

The night continued; it didn't matter whether it was truly nighttime or not as far as they were concerned. Stu, Clint, Skip, and Dana strolled the casino complexes for what seemed like hours without ever seeing a window or door that revealed the truth of daylight. One of the ladies, likely turned off by Skip's marriage gripe or Clint's free drink crack, had bailed, so three women accompanied the four Vegas-bachelors. Clint found a cigar kiosk and purchased four Churchills, passing them around. With slowly burning stogies, three lovely ladies, and Dana's music thumping to help them keep step, the party moved through the halls of the interconnected casinos—they weren't even sure which casino they were in at the moment—as they laughed and flirted and floated.

Eventually, they exited the casino complex and reentered real time. Like cave-dwellers freshly emerged from the shadows, or Portlanders visiting Laguna Beach, they squinted at the sunlight.

"I can't believe it," Skip said. "It's, like, daytime!"

"Middle of the day," Dana said, judging by the position of the sun above. He pulled the phone from his pocket and confirmed that it was half past 11.

"High noon," Clint said with a laughter-filled grunt. He almost looked like a haggard gunslinger, minus the gun.

"Well, it's always midnight somewhere," one of the ladies said. Was it Lucy or Barb? Stu couldn't remember which was which. It wasn't because they were so alike. He couldn't think clearly. Stu and his friends had been at it for nearly 24 hours straight. In fact, Stu wondered how they were still going strong with such energy. It seemed they had all caught a second wind when they took their places at Caesar's roulette table, accompanied by the sociable women. Was it because the presence of the ladies gave them new resolve, or had one of them slipped something into their drinks to keep them going? Was Stu becoming paranoid or delirious because of too much alcohol or not enough sleep? *Just because you're paranoid doesn't mean they're not after you*—was that R.E.M. or Pearl Jam or Nirvana? Stu was wide awake in their middle-of-the-night center of the day, but he just couldn't think straight.

Skip seemed to share the sentiment. "Everything seems backwards or out of place."

"How so?" Dana asked.

"Not just that it seems like the middle of the night even though it's really the middle of the day—"

Clint jumped in. "Or that you're middle-aged but you're acting like you're teen-aged?"

"Not funny," Skip said. He looked back at Stu. "I mean, aren't we having this bachelor's party a little early? Everything seems backwards."

"There's no time like the present," Dana said. "Besides, this won't end here. We'll get together then, too."

Clint nodded. "You know we'll have a good time then."

The daytime traffic was as relentless as the nighttime traffic, stop and go. The lights made the vehicles sit idle as frequently as it allowed them to move forward. The continuing music from Dana's shoulder bag did battle with the open-window car stereos that bounced in place. Cheering and music came from a hotel swim party where a radio station seemed to be broadcasting live.

"Let's get back to the situation at hand," Dana said in a silky voice. "What do you young ladies want to do?"

Lucy and Barb looked at one another and smiled. "How about a proper drink, at a proper bar?"

"Yeah, no more of that watered-down casino juice," said the third, Charlene.

"Sounds like a plan," Dana agreed.

In the distance ahead, a loud screech gave them pause, followed by a jolting metal-against-metal crash and grind. Stu stopped, focused, and saw the car accident in the distance. "Let's check it out," he said, picking up his pace.

The others followed behind him. Dana was tempted to change songs to something more suspenseful; this dash to the scene felt more "Eye of the Tiger" than "Chariots of Fire." Within moments, they were beside the accident that clogged traffic on the strip: a Rolls Royce had slammed into the back of a Toyota Corolla. It had happened only moments ago, and the two drivers were already out of their cars, screaming at each other on the side of the road. The Japanese man in an expensive suit complained about the front of his Rolls, and a dressed-down man with a British accent cursed about the back of his Toyota.

"I've seen a lot of accidents," Stu said, "But I've never seen a Rolls in a collision. At least, not in person."

"You're sick," Clint said, relighting the ashy end of Skip's half-consumed cigar and commandeering it for himself. His was long gone, as were Stu's and Dana's.

"We'll *all* be sick when we wake up from this dream," Skip said.

"Speak for yourself," Clint said. "I don't plan to go to sleep anytime soon." He grinned at the woman beside him.

The police arrived and began taking reports from the two drivers and others who had witnessed the accident. Everyone was focused intently on their versions of the truth. Stu inched closer to the wreckage, taking in the details: broken glass of the Rolls windshield, buckled metal of the hood, the cracked plastic tail lights of the Toyota and the broken-off back fender. The hood ornament from the Rolls. By the looks of it, this would be a two-tow job. Impatient drivers honked in the far-off distance, unaware of what was stalling traffic. Stu looked around, making sure that no one was watching, and knelt down.

"Emily," Stu whispered. She was beautiful, despite the rough gray blemish to the side of her face where her polished cheek of stainless steel had scraped the asphalt. She stood about three inches tall on a round pedestal, bent over, arms behind her like wings, looking as though she were ready to fly—to fly through the air on the front of a beautiful car. Again, Stu looked around at the drivers speaking passionately with the police officers. He scooped up the hood ornament, placing it in the front pocket of his knit slacks where it bulged like too many keys.

"What's he doing?" Barb asked.

"That's just Stu being Stu," Clint said. "A real sicko."

"Just look at that," Stu said, standing again on the sidewalk with the others, looking at the scene before them. "It's not often you see a fine vehicle like that in an accident like this."

"Who would want to?" Lucy asked.

Dana smoothed out the situation. "Gentleman's got an unusual hobby, that's all."

"Like I said," Clint said, "The guy's wacko."

Skip asked, "Are you really going to walk with that?"

Stu grinned. "I know for a fact that the insurance company will have to pay for a new one anyway. She's damaged goods, destined for a scrap pile. I'm rescuing her."

At the bar, the seven of them pushed into a round booth in the bar's again-night atmosphere and enjoyed some Tequila Sunrises, at the request of Lucy, the girl who seemed to be fixated on Stu.

"So, you collect hood ornaments?" She placed her hand on the ornament, bulging from his pocket. "Kind of a weird hobby."

"Oh," Clint grunted, "it's weirder than that."

Stu smiled. "I collect pieces from wrecks. And ruins."

Lucy scrunched her face. "You collect wreckage?"

Skip laughed. "In more ways than one."

"Just look at this," Stu said, pulling out the hood ornament. "It's called Spirit of Ecstasy."

"I've experienced that before," Lucy joked. "Got any?"

Stu ignored her second question, still focused on the first. "There are thousands of these, but only *one* like this—only one with *this* blemish, *this* unique quality, only one that had *this* experience, the wreck that we saw out there."

Clint slurped his drink, then slammed it back to the table. "He's got some doozies. Hood ornaments. Chunks of car grill grids. Tire slices. Fiberglass shards from bodies. Oily engine parts. You name it."

Stu continued. "This may be the only Spirit of Ecstasy to be in a wreck and scrape her face on the Vegas strip. Ever."

Dana looked from the hood ornament to the flesh-and-blood girls. "Beauty's in the eye of the beholder."

Stu shook his head. "It's not about beauty. It's about reality. About history and experience. About honesty. If you can appreciate the beauty in a wreck or in the remains of a burned-down rowhouse shell or in the ruins of an ancient building, then you can appreciate—or tolerate—just about anything."

# VENICE IN VEGAS

Dana had his arm around Barb in the shadowy bar booth. "How do you girls feel about a hot tub in an Italian statue garden?"

"That sounds lovely," Barb said, sucking the dregs of her Tequila Sunrise with a straw.

"Let's do it, then." Dana stood. In a moment, the group was back on their feet, out on the strip, walking toward The Venetian.

"We didn't even really need the hotel suite," Skip said. "We didn't stay there."

Charlene smiled. "Oh, we may find some use for it yet." Skip blushed, Clint laughed out loud, Dana shifted the musical selection to something smoother, and Stu led the way back to their hotel. They were not hung over only because they were still drunk, still in the midst of their extended night on the town. That, and possibly whatever speed or euphoric drugs had been slipped into their drinks.

"Relaxing in the hot tub sounds like just the ticket," Stu said. "Let's go slip into our swimwear." The party of seven walked through the halls of The Venetian, Frank Sinatra crooning on Dana's loudspeaker. They swaggered—almost in slow motion—into an elevator with an old couple in face shields—probably in their 70s—and sensed their unease as the elevator doors closed around them. Four drunken and hyped-up men, a loud speaker blaring (at least it was Frank Sinatra instead of Big Sean this time), and three half-drunk women who were dressed as though they weren't sure whether their jobs involved waiting tables, dancing on tables, or a little bit of both.

Dana smiled at the old man and woman, up against the wall at the far corner of the elevator. "Nice day, isn't it?"

The woman held her tongue. The man nodded. "It certainly looks that way." She nudged him. The elevator door opened and they got off. Stu, Dana, Skip, Clint, Lucy, Charlene, and Barb rode it closer to the top.

The women seemed impressed with their suite. "I think I could live here," Charlene said.

"You ladies make yourselves comfortable," Dana said.

Clint pointed to the stocked bar. "Make yourselves some drinks."

Charlene, Barb, and Lucy walked to the bar while the guys went to the three bedrooms and bathroom to change.

When Stu came back out in his swimming trunks and a tee-shirt, he found the three ladies and three guys standing at the wall of windows, looking out at the strip below. Clint yelled, "Grab yourself a drink, Stu, while the grabbing's good."

Stu picked up one of the remaining screwdrivers and joined them at the window. "Are we ready for the hot tub?"

Dana smirked. "We were just discussing our dilemma."

Charlene said, "We ain't got our bathing suits."

Dana chuckled. "I told them they could just wear their underwear in the hot tub. It's almost the same thing."

"No-wear is fine, too," Clint threw in.

Skip gave Clint a push. "I don't think they're buying it, dude."

"But ladies," Stu said. "You don't want to miss the Venetian statue gardens. Quite beautiful. It's like you're in Italy."

"Well, all right," Lucy agreed. The party left the suite—barware in hand yet again—and they made their way down to the first floor, where outdoor street cafes filled fake indoor squares and a canal carried gondolas along crystal-clear water, the standing gondoliers serenading seated couples in love.

Skip fretted, even in his drunken stupor. "Think they're gonna bill us for all the glasses we keep taking out of the room?"

"Who cares," Clint asked. "It's only money."

"Yeah," Skip barked, "And you're working multiple jobs just to make ends meet with it."

"Don't worry so much," Clint said. "We'll manage. Right now, focus on right now."

Dana had forgotten to pump up the music—or more likely, Stu figured, his batteries had finally crashed, as they were destined to do soon enough. The serenading gondoliers filled the silence with their Italian love songs. They stood upon the back ends of their gondolas in striped black and white shirts, red scarves, and punting poles in their hands. Lucy pulled on Stu's arm. "Can we ride one of those?"

Stu shrugged. "Why not?" He escorted Lucy down the steps to one of the waiting vessels.

Dana looked at the other two. "Who else wants to be taken for a ride?"

Charlene and Barb looked at one another. Charlene said, "I'm game." Dana escorted Charlene down the steps to the canal's edge.

"I'm not interested," Skip said, not wanting to get entangled with these girls beyond their company, and not wanting to spend money on the ride.

"Suits me," Barb shrugged. "Let's follow alongside them."

They did. Stu and Dana took their companions on individual gondolas, each of their watermen serenading while the other took a breath so that the sounds of their romantic songs filled their cruises. The canal passed from under the fake blue sky inside, to under the true blue sky outside. They lost Clint, Skip, and Barb momentarily, as they had to cross a bridge and pass through a door to find the canal on the other side.

"That was nice," Lucy said. "Now let's take a dip."

"Ladies and gentlemen," Dana extended his arm, "To the Italian gardens."

# HINDSIGHT HOT TUB

Stu moaned. "This feels wonderful." He relaxed in the hot tub, looking up at the Italian gardens, statues, and fountains all around them, etched crystal drink in hand, Lucy soaking beside him, surrounded by his best friends and a few new ones.

"It's an absolute delight," Charlene agreed. She looked up at Barb. "You should get in." Barb shook her head, refusing to undress. She sat on the ledge with her bare legs and feet in the water. Venus or some other beauty carved of marble stood at the other end of the hot tub, making it a symmetrical scene. Four middle-aged men in the hot tub, two younger women between them, and two beauties outside the tub at either end, green orange trees and bushes all about. They relaxed in their own little paradise.

"So, Stu," Skip asked. "Do you think you'll be able to adjust to your new lifestyle? After the ceremony?"

Clint crunched a piece of ice from his screwdriver between his teeth. "That's a stupid question."

"Playboy ways die hard," Dana said, his arm wrapped around the waist of Charlene. "But they're a cinch to pick back up."

Skip appeared troubled, despite his place in a hot tub with friends and playmates. "I don't know, guys. I still feel like Stu might be making a mistake."

"You never know for sure," Dana said. "I mean, hindsight's 20/20."

Stu laughed. "Guess this is the year when everything is supposed to become clear."

Dana frowned. "Come again?"

"I mean, the year is 2020. Time for hindsight to come out into the forefront. Everything should be in perfect focus."

As though trying to wrap their impaired minds around that, everyone grew quiet. Stu closed his eyes, hearing and feeling the bubbles and flesh all around him, drifting.

As he allowed the hot tub to relax him, Stu thought back. Things had certainly seemed to be in perfect focus back in 2004, the year that Skip got married to Leona. Back then, at 34, Stu knew that he was destined to be single, that being true to himself meant being faithful to no one else in matters of love. Clint had already married Amanda nearly twenty years prior to that—he'd gotten her pregnant and dropped out of high school to do the honorable thing—and then Skip, also 34, was going to punish himself with the same life sentence.

Back then, in 2004, Stu returned to Northern Virginia for the first time since his high school days, having already moved to York, Pennsylvania. A year after Skip and Leona's wedding, Stu moved to Baltimore.

Something bugged Stu about Skip's intent to marry this girl he had met only a few months before. Skip had always been naïve, and Stu didn't want to see his friend crushed. Now, in hindsight, Stu could recognize some selfishness in his concerns about his friend's marriage—that he was the last of his high school buddies to remain single. Back then, he was sure that marriage was the wrong choice for himself, Skip, Clint, or anyone who knew what was best for them.

Stu had enjoyed his life of perpetual bachelorhood back in those days. But again, in hindsight, he realized now that it was more that he enjoyed being pseudo-miserable. Stu loved the hunt of romance, the quick thrill, the one-night stand or two-month relationship. But he had convinced himself that it was for his own pleasure and contentment that he broke things off (if the girl didn't beat him to it) before things got too serious, that he wanted to keep it light. Seeing Skip and Leona so sappily but genuinely in love with each other in 2004 had given Stu pause. Was he really being protective of Skip, or of his own potential heartache?

Something else buzzing all around them in 2004, like an almost-hangover that was there but not noticed unless focused upon, was the overbearing love songs of the cicadas. Brood X had reemerged, and they were in full force during Skip and Leona's outdoor wedding. Stu remembered how unreal everything was—the marrying off of his most-unlikely-to-succeed-with-women friend, the foreign invasion of these insects he'd not seen since another awkward time of his life, when he was in high school.

As Stu drove into the wooded hills of northern Virginia, his windows rolled down to enjoy the warm summer air cooled only by his speed, the uncanny noise had started soft and dull, nearly unnoticeable. Like a clock you know is going to chime in a few minutes and ruin your conversation, but passes unnoticed, there but unregistered. As Stu drove closer to the wedding, it was as though the clock struck 24. The sound of the cicadas grew louder and fuller, an incessant screeching.

By the time he'd reached his destination, it was unearthly, a crescendo from nature, unnatural. It was an eerie alien landscape, a scene from an old 1950s bug-eyed monster movie with sound effects so bizarre they couldn't possibly be real. But this sound was real. For Stu, this sound and feeling came to epitomize the weekend, to represent love itself.

Stu's thoughts drifted along memories as his arms and legs drifted weightlessly in the hot tub. Sure, Stu had experienced Brood X before. He remembered in 1987, when he had moved to Virginia to go to high school. He'd bonded with Clint, Skip, and Dana over cardboard pizza and card games in the school cafeteria. Not long after their friendship began, Clint had fallen for Amanda, one of the cheerleaders. He'd gotten her pregnant and decided to do what he thought was the honorable thing. He dropped out of high school to marry her. Clint and Amanda were still together nearly 34 years later and had three adult children to show for it. But they'd gotten married for the wrong reasons, to Stu's way of thinking.

Stu had been graced with the best marriage models, at least in his pre-teen years: his parents; his grandparents on both sides; three sets of aunts and uncles; a number of family friends. So many older people he knew had been happily married for a long time. But from the perspective of a teen in 1987 or even as a thirtysomething in 2004, they were all *older* people—in their forties and fifties and sixties—and didn't really *live* their lives as much as merely exist in them. Not to mention that almost half of those long-lasting relationships—his parents' included—eventually ended in separation or divorce.

When Skip was going to tie the knot in 2004, Stu had convinced himself that he was living the high life, that he was enjoying his long-lived bachelorhood, and that marriage was little more than a white flag, giving up and conforming to what was expected of a proper, upstanding citizen. But bearing witness to the second of his best friends from high school being married off caused Stu to question the merits of his own bachelorhood.

Now that Stu was in his fifties, he had even more reason to question his younger assumptions. Stu wasn't the same fifty-something that fifty-somethings had been fifty years ago. But maybe that's what fifty-somethings said fifty years ago. Maybe sitting drunk in a hot tub with some girls they just met wasn't the pinnacle of middle-aged success he would have thought it to be twenty years ago. Hugh Heffner had been able to pull it off, but Hugh Heffner was a reality show before there were reality shows. This was reality. Despite his hope to be hip, Stu would probably be more at home if he were literally at home than he was here in this Las Vegas cesspool.

Back in 2004, Stu had stumbled onto the idea that romance was like the cycle of a cicada. You could count on a few weeks, perhaps a couple of months, of excited buzz—liveliness, romance, excitement, attraction, mating—and then, a seventeen-year sleep; a lapse into monotony and routine that had no way of living up to the promise of the noisy romance at the start.

He realized this concept was fed by a combination of his friend's naïve commitment to marriage in 2004, and the droning infestation all around them—not to mention the association with Stu's first feelings of true love in his relationship with Skye back in 1987, the last time the cicadas had emerged.

With this understanding of romantic love, Stu was wise enough, even in 2004, to know it made sense not to get attached. To settle down with one woman was to settle. Stu understood that if he committed himself to one woman, gone would be the highs of discovering the things you love about a person, gone would be the romantic thrills of budding romance. Here to stay would be bored compliance and mundane routine. *Yes, Hon, I'll get milk on the way home from work. Sure, Hon, let's binge watch "Curb Your Enthusiasm's" newest season. Fine, Hon, let's go see that chirpy rom-com this weekend.* Why subject yourself to that when you could remain single, swinging from one buzzing romance to another?

But, even back in 2004, seeing Amanda and Clint still making it work 17 years in and watching Skip and Leona together, so alike they were like twin copies of the same person, male and female, made Stu begin to question his Cicada-Romance Theory. Had he been fooling himself? Did Skip and Clint have it right? Was Stu going nowhere fast, fleeing the inevitable lush green lawn and white picket fence? At 34, Stu had found himself beginning to question his playboy lifestyle, found himself considering a conversion to the lifestyle Clint and Skip had chosen. Perhaps it was time for Stu to slow down and not be in such a hurry for the next thrill. Maybe the time had come to join his friends in the good life.

By the time the cicadas had died in the summer of 2004, so had Stu's momentary notion. Stu knew who he was and knew what he believed. And maybe that was why his life now—in 2020—was a wreck that he could barely hold together, a Toyota Corolla with a fallen-off fender whose only prospect for greatness was to be kissed by the Spirit of Ecstasy before falling to the asphalt.

All of Stu's friends—except Dana—were married now. But did that mean Stu should be, too?

# WHERE TIFFANY CAME IN

Just a season after Skip and Leona's wedding, shortly after moving to Baltimore, Tiffany had entered the picture. It was autumn of 2004. Stu went to free concerts around town a couple times each week as a way to get acquainted with different areas of his new city, and because he loved music. He went to so many concerts and saw so many acts that he couldn't remember most of them. Some of them seemed to make the rounds and played often: Scrambled Legs, June Star, B'More Loud, Kelly Bell Band, The Uke Troop, Laughing Colors, The Back Porch Rockers, Red Sammy. At some events, Skip would be fortunate enough to catch the eye of a girl who caught his eye, and he'd ask her out for a drink before asking for more.

One girl in particular often showed up at the same concerts that Stu enjoyed. Not every concert, but enough of them that he spotted her in the dancing crowd three or four times a month, recognized her as a music lover like himself. She had caught his eye without even knowing it; he had some difficulty getting her attention. One day, while the Back Porch Rockers were doing a cover of the Robyn Hitchcock song, "So You Think You're in Love," he made his way through the semi-dancing-in-place crowd to semi-dance in the place next to her. They made eye contact, and she smiled shyly at him as though she knew his intentions, then looked back at the band. Before that concert in Baltimore's Inner Harbor was over, she'd already danced her way out of sight and Stu ended up at a bar in Fells Point where he picked up another girl that he knew he wouldn't ask out for seconds.

Stu had started his career with a job in York, Pennsylvania at a local Allstate franchise. There, he began his work as an insurance adjuster. Before long, he found a better-paying job in more-populated Baltimore with a local company, *Wreck of the Hesperus Insurance Agency*. His new employer allowed him to do inspections and appraisals himself, in addition to doing the claims work in the office. Stu had long been interested in ruins and wreckage, would have happily become a professional grave robber or rubberneck ambulance chaser if there had been a way to make it pay. But it was during these post-accident vehicle inspections required by his new Baltimore job that he'd developed his interest in photography. Somehow, the details of a cracked grill, torn tire, pelleted glass, or ripped fiberglass fender looked rawer, more intense, more meaningful on film, in close-up, than up close and in person with the naked eye.

Stu had an appointment to inspect a car in Mount Vernon, along Read Street, one Thursday afternoon. He got there for the 5 p.m. appointment with his Nikon camera, met the man who'd had the wreck and was probably at fault, and photographed the details: broken off driver's side mirror, scraped-into-the-metal door, scratches on the back fender. He finished up at 5:30 as the free concert right around the corner near the Washington Monument—the first Washington Monument designed by the same architect who designed the one in DC—was gearing up to begin at six. Camera bag on his shoulder, he grabbed a Resurrection Ale at the nearby booth and claimed a spot on the green, right in front of the makeshift stage.

Scrambled Legs, a local band who couldn't quite crack the top 40 except for one hit they'd collaborated on with a poet years ago, burst into a combination of covers and originals that sounded pretty good to Stu. He wasn't the only one who dug the sound, Stu realized, as a large crowd had gathered around and behind him. Within that crowd: the mesmerizing woman he had tried to dance up to at the Inner Harbor concerts.

During a cover of R.E.M.'s "Turn You Inside Out," Stu slyly danced his way toward the woman with the long, blonde hair. She wore a light blouse that revealed her bra beneath, and a tight skirt that went halfway to her knees. She sported flats, but she certainly wasn't. "I've seen you before," he said.

She smiled at him and looked at his camera bag, slung over his short-sleeve button down shirt, which was untucked, flowing over a pair of slate-hued slacks. His shirt had been tucked in when he was on the job. Fortunately, *Wreck of the Hesperus Insurance* no longer required him to wear their uniform polo shirts with a ship emerging from the water on the breast. "Are you with the band?" she asked, motioning to his camera.

"What? Oh, no. I'm ... just getting off work. Didn't have time to drop this off."

"Me, too," she said. "Just got off work." She glanced to the stage. "Legs are pretty good."

Stu looked at her legs and was ready to agree, then realized she was referring to the band. "Anyone who can do justice to old-school R.E.M. is fine by me."

When they exchanged names, Stu initiated a handshake—not to be formal, but because he wanted an excuse to put Tiffany's soft hand in his. The band shifted into a rendition of Counting Crows' "Raining in Baltimore," and Tiffany half-sang along. "… I need a big love… I need a phone call…"

Stu wanted to give her the phone call, could even have been persuaded to offer her a big love. But first, as the Scrambled Legs concert was gearing down, Stu offered to escort her to the drink tent for a beer.

"Mind if we get a drink somewhere else?" she asked. "I prefer my wine in a glass."

"Let's do it." Stu balanced his red plastic cup like a brick on the pyramid atop the overflowing trash can. The towering Washington Monument to their back and the band behind them, they walked along Charles Street and came upon Mick O'Sheay's Pub. An Irish band that was every bit as good as the concert outside filled the room of wood and glass with harmonica and guitar. During the set, Stu sipped beer and watched Tiffany sip wine. After the set, the two talked.

Stu explained to Tiffany that no, he was not an artist, that he took pictures to document accidents for insurance claims. She explained to him that she wasn't an artist either, she worked at Mercy Hospital on St. Paul, but she adored art generally and the Barbizon painters from the late 1800s and early 1900s in particular, especially the works of Charles-Francois Daubigny and H.C. Delpy. Her favorite musician was Robyn Hitchcock and his favorite band was R.E.M., and each appreciated the other's musical tastes; they both enjoyed music of all kinds, particularly agreeing on James Hunter and Frank Zappa and Leonard Cohen and Tom Waits. They both had an affinity for pop music pretending to be "alternative" from the 1990s and 2000s and new artists who played real instruments. Music seemed to be their most common ground, not to speak of raw attraction for one another, so they agreed to meet at an outdoor June Star concert the following week. Just after she agreed, the Irish band resumed, announcing themselves as the Donegal X-Press, and they managed to overpower the applause with a harmonica riff and guitar.

The following week, after the June Star show at Belvedere Square, they headed for the square's wine bar and got to know one another better. Opening up, wanting to create intimacy, he confided to her the difficulty of seeing his parent's marriage die before him and she topped that by describing the heart-wrenching scene of witnessing a couple process the reality of a stillborn in the delivery room. Their conversation took a more cheerful turn when a Grateful Dead song came from the wine bar's speaker system and they reminisced about the times each of them had almost seen the Dead in concert, she in New York and he in Ohio.

Stu asked Tiffany to come home with him to his row-house apartment on Elrino Street in east Baltimore and she refused. She wouldn't do that, not so soon, but she would like to go out with him again. "Maybe on a proper date this time," she'd suggested. At their table in the wine bar in Belvedere Square, after the June Star concert, Stu asked her if she would consider the upcoming R.E.M show at the Daughters of the

American Revolution Constitution Hall in DC a "proper date."

She smiled and looked into her drink, answering him as though talking to herself. "He's got pretty persuasion."

So, they'd already been out together on several occasions—outdoor concerts and after-show bars—before their "first date." Their official first date, as Tiffany referred to it, was when Stu picked Tiffany up at her Mount Vernon apartment, her standing in front of what looked like an 1800s rowhouse mansion, and drove her through miles, music, and conversation to Washington, DC's DAR Constitution Hall, near the White House.

In his mid-forties, Michael Stipe was an animated and limber man with staying power—not just based on his long career, but on his long set of songs illustrated by his jumping and twisting and dancing with more elasticity and energy than Stu thought possible for men of a certain age. (That's what Stu had thought when he was in his 30s, at the concert with Tiffany. Thinking back to it now, Stu had to remind himself that he had reached his fifties—he'd have to reconsider what "old" meant yet again, and he wondered at what age he'd relent and just admit *he* was old.)

Back at that November 2004 show, part of R.E.M.'s "Vote for Change" tour, lights flashed, music blared, and Stu was even pleased to discover the answer to a question he'd not yet dared to breach with Tiffany—that she, too, was in agreement with his political views. As Bill Clinton had proclaimed a decade-plus earlier, as R.E.M. proclaimed now, it was time for change. Stu didn't wear his politics on his sleeve and certainly would not have let political views ruin his chance for a short-term relationship with this amazing woman. But the fact that she, too, was voting for Kerry over Bush made him feel as great as the show did. He wouldn't know it at the time, but that would be his last R.E.M. concert—the last concert R.E.M. would perform in the DC area before the band would break up in 2011—but it would certainly not be the last time he went out with Tiffany. They wouldn't break up in 2011 the way Stu's favorite band had, and they wouldn't break up anytime shortly after that. In fact, they hadn't broken up yet.

After the "Vote for Change" show, after the election showed that the show would not change the vote or the President, Stu and Tiffany continued dating. Neither had committed to an exclusive relationship—they weren't children and they weren't "going steady" or making anything official—but Stu had certainly set his sights on her and only her, at least for the moment. He hadn't abandoned his cicada-love theory and imagined that their relationship would heat up to supernova status soon and eventually—maybe in a year, maybe in a few—burn out and leave them both better human beings for the experience. But even with that theory intact, his focus was her.

For their next big date, aside from the regular meet-up concerts at the Inner Harbor, Mount Vernon Square, Belvedere Square, and in downtown Towson, Stu got tickets to the Robyn Hitchcock show at the 9:30 club. Once again, he drove her to DC, enjoying the ride and the conversation with her as much as the show itself. They got there early enough that they had to wait to get in, so they waited at the underground bar, sort of a Crayola-crayon colored box in the ground, where they got drinks (beer and wine) and waited for an escort up to the main floor.

They managed to stake out spots standing in the front row, so close that they could lean on the metal scaffolding beneath the stage when they weren't standing straight up and dancing. This old man (again, age didn't quite compute in Stu's current-day mind) really rocked the house, displaying a Michael-Stipe-like energy that surprised Stu and made him appreciate the British punk artist even more than he had when he'd only heard him on audio recordings. Those same recordings took on a new meaning now, after seeing him live. After that brilliant show, after another drink at a nearby pub, after the drive home from DC to Mount Vernon, Tiffany finally invited Stu up to her apartment.

Inside the Mount Vernon mansion, the massive staircase shocked Stu. You could have gotten an extra apartment on each floor had that staircase been replaced with a normal-sized flight. Likewise, he discovered that when she said that she, like him, lived in a rowhouse apartment, she had an entirely different picture of what that meant. Hers was a modern, luxury apartment inside this historic mansion, a roomy two-bedroom flat with a bath and a half, nice-sized kitchen, living room, dining room, and even a small balcony with room for two chairs and a wine table between. She retrieved a bottle of red and two glasses. He offered to open it, but she said she was perfectly capable, that she pulled things from tight places for a living.

Stu took his glass of wine and enjoyed the light balcony breeze. "What, like removing catheters? Bet you hear a lot of screams."

Tiffany grinned. "Well, I do get an earful of screaming on a regular basis. But not from withdrawing catheters. From helping deliver babies."

"Are you a midwife?"

"I'm a doctor."

Stu smiled. "That's amazing," he said.

"What, that a woman like me could be a doctor?"

"No," Stu clarified. "That *I'm* seeing a woman who is a doctor. You were already the perfect package. But now I find out that you help people for a living. That you have one of the most noble professions on earth. Wow."

"I put my pants on one leg at a time, just like you and everyone else."

"Yeah but …" Stu drew close to her, placed his wine glass on the table, and proceeded to kiss her. They had kissed good-night before, but this was different, better. This was a kiss hello. They kissed long enough that they nearly lost their trains of thought. He pulled back and looked her in her blue eyes. They twinkled in the starlight in a way that he didn't realize happened outside romance novels and rom-coms. Stu regained his train of thought. "Yeah, but … I'm more interested in how you take them off."

"Come again?"

"Your pants. You put them on one leg at a time, but—"

"I really like you, Stu. I want us to keep seeing each other. But I'm not ready for that yet."

Stu backed away. "I can respect that." He forced himself to say the words, trying to actually mean them despite his raging desire. He retrieved his glass of Bordeaux and sipped. "So, you're a doctor at Mercy."

"Well, for now. I'm hoping to move to an OB/GYN private practice soon. I'm actually a perinatologist."

"A peri-what now?

"I specialize in prenatal and at-birth abnormalities. A pretty specific area. But for now, in the early stage of my career, I'm working in the maternity ward. Paying my dues."

"Very nice," Stu said, both to her and as a summary of their evening together.

# IMPERFECT MATCH

Stu and Tiffany continued to be a comfortably compatible match, if an imperfect one. They loved spending time together, taking in concerts, and going out to dinner. Tiffany took Stu to the Walters Art Museum and Baltimore Museum of Art, where they saw works by Daubigny and Delpy and photographs of ancient ruins as well as artifacts strikingly similar to ruins themselves. Stu took Tiffany to the remains of a dilapidated building in Baltimore's inner city, the doors boarded up, the windows broken by the thrown rocks of neighborhood teens, charred bricks falling from the side where the neighboring home had been burnt down and then torn away, holes in that bare side exposing the decaying remains of the interior rooms—rooms that once held life, nurtured families, kept them safe.

"This is weird," Tiffany said, looking around, uncomfortable.

"Don't worry," Stu said, "we're perfectly safe. I come to places like this all the time."

"Really odd."

"I don't think so." He snapped a few pictures. "Seeing places like this, in this condition, reminds me of how fragile life is. How insecure security really is. How fleeting a moment—or a life—can be. Everything we think of as permanent, as 'the norm' or 'how it is' is just in our head. It's all temporary. In 100 years, my place and your place might look like this. You and I? We'll look a lot worse."

"Are you afraid of what you will become? Of being broken, or decaying? Oh, God, listen to myself."

"No, because we're all broken to some degree already."

"What's the point? Focusing on damaged goods? Wouldn't you rather photograph some flowers or trees? Something nice?"

"The point? Don't waste time waiting for flowers to grow. Don't settle for good enough. Go for what you want, live your life the way you want to live it, be you. I think seeing ruins and accidents reminds me how important it is to protect what you want and love and what you value."

He'd planned to take her to his apartment after the excursion to this shell of a rowhouse, but doing so didn't seem right, given her reaction to what was for him a passion. He didn't want to freak her out. Instead, they went to Ottobar for a performance by Kilowatt Hours, then back to her place. He played his part and acted on his wishes, advancing. She played her part and averted his advances, settling for heavy petting and kissing. They were both satisfied for the moment.

But Stu knew he couldn't keep Tiffany at bay forever. He invited her to his rowhouse apartment on Elrino Street one Sunday afternoon. She knew the area because Hopkins' Bayview Campus and its state-of-the-art trauma center were right next door, along with the research labs of the National Institutes of Health, where she'd once considered a government career in prenatal research, given her subspecialty. Bayview, or Joseph Lee, was a stable, somewhat gentrifying blue-collar neighborhood where whites, blacks, Asians, and Hispanics, doctors, nurses, construction workers, and office workers mingled and coexisted. There were small rowhouse apartments and tall rowhouse redesigns with third floors and rooftop decks added on. People sat on their porches and children played ball and Frisbee and lawn darts in the front yards.

Stu's apartment made up the first floor and finished basement of one of these old, orange-bricked homes: a bedroom, living room, and office on the first floor, an eat-in kitchen, bathroom, and storage area in the finished basement.

In the living room, besides the sofa, chair, and television, were framed posters of the Roman Colosseum; Delphi, Greece; and Taos, New Mexico. In his bedroom, framed photographs of Chichen Itza's pyramid and ruins. In a series of six photographs along one wall, a shadow resembling a snake was tracked, slithering down the steps of the ancient pyramid.

"Did you take these?" Tiffany asked.

Stu nodded.

"They're beautiful."

In Stu's office, the expected wooden desk, with file cabinet drawers, sat covered in bills and folders. Two bookshelves filled only partially with books, mostly with pieces he'd collected: hood ornaments, shavings of metal, shards of glass, and pieces barely recognizable as remains of automobile accidents. Also on the shelves, rocks, worn-away bricks, sea glass, and driftwood. Framed photographs in the office depicted close-ups of automobile accidents—twisted metal, the parts and pieces of cars intertwined, shattered windshields, vehicles bent like horseshoes, jackknifed tractor trailers. No bodies, no blood, and nothing gory. Reluctantly, Tiffany admitted that she sensed something artistic in these photographs, something oddly alluring that caused confusion to spill over her face.

"Yes," Stu answered the unasked question that was undeniably there between them. "I took these ones too. Funny thing is, people aren't as quick to say they're beautiful. But they are! How are the broken down and decaying ruins of old buildings so appealing, but modern marvels in distress are so troubling?"

"Good point," Tiffany admitted. "I don't know the answer to that."

Stu led Tiffany downstairs to his large eat-in kitchen, where he took two wine glasses from the cabinet and poured them two glasses of Merlot. "Let me show you the rest of my collection."

From the kitchen, Stu opened the door and pulled a chain light. In the storage area were dozens and dozens of untreated wooden shelves, broken only by the washer, dryer, and oil tank responsible for heating the home. The shelves were covered with artifacts from auto accidents. Countless hood ornaments and grill grid pieces, seat belt buckles and car grill emblems, gas caps and hub cap fragments, nuts, bolts, hoses, belts, and spark plugs, engine parts and carburetors broken down to their most elemental parts. Another shelf included glass and bricks and railing post fragments and house numbers and mailbox flags and faucets and spouts and calcified shower heads and gutter sections and roof shingles from houses, some burnt, some worn, some looking to be hundreds of years old. On the wall above the oil tank hung bent street signs and stop signs and railroad crossing signs, bent fence poles and charred, corrugated metal.

"It's something else," Tiffany said, not knowing what else to say.

"Don't worry, I'm not weird," he said. "I'm just honest. This is interesting stuff. This is art every bit as fascinating as some framed detail prints or tchotchkes you can buy at Wal-Mart or Target."

"I get it," Tiffany said. "I just didn't expect it."

Stu laughed. "I didn't expect you to expect it. But I'm glad that you get it. To be honest, I didn't expect you to get it, either."

"I get it because I get you," Tiffany said. "Word of advice." She looked around her with wide eyes. "Don't ever bring a girl that you like down here until you get to charm her first. Because if I had seen this on date one, there wouldn't have been a date two."

Uncharacteristically, Stu found himself wondering why Tiffany would even bring up another hypothetical girl. For now, he was as focused on her as he was his collection. More focused on her. He was glad he hadn't framed or displayed any of the photographs he'd taken of her at concerts and on the street. That might have thrown her off.

# SOME ASSEMBLY REQUIRED

Stu had learned long ago that sometimes you could not put two things you loved together. For example, Stu loved hot pizza and he loved fresh pineapple, but he detested Hawaiian pizza. He loved his mother and he loved his father, but he hated rare moments when the two of them existed in the same room together.

There were other things that Stu knew did not belong together, but when they were forced together, they resulted in an interesting beauty. For example, when a stuntman on a motorcycle attempted and failed to jump a wide line of old cars, crashing down into them and causing a pattern uniquely its own. Or when two people from very different backgrounds with somewhat different interests were attracted to each other and formed the perfect couple—or better yet, an imperfect couple that held together like two pieces of metal spiraled together, forged in fire.

So when Stu found out about the upcoming concert at Ram's Head in Annapolis, he knew he'd found the best possible meshing of his and Tiffany's musical sensibilities. He'd decided to surprise her.

"Where are we headed?" Tiffany had asked. "DAR? Wolftrap? Hamilton Theater?"

"You'll see," Stu said coolly.

"Why won't you tell me?"

"Because I want you to be surprised."

She looked out the window, playfully impatient. "I should have looked in the City Paper and online. I didn't know you were going to surprise me with a concert, so I didn't think to look."

"Just the way I planned it."

She took stock of their location. "Wait, we're not headed to DC?"

"Nope."

"Where are we going? Ocean City? Annapolis?"

"That's right. Annapolis."

"That must mean Ram's Head." She pulled out her smartphone.

"Put that away!"

She laughed and put her phone away. He'd tried to keep it a surprise, so she relented and stayed with him instead of on a "which-hunt." She would figure out which act they were seeing soon enough.

They pulled into Annapolis and he parked along the street far enough away that they would have to walk along the water, past St. Ann's Church at the center of the circle, and up to Ram's Head. They'd both been to the venue before, but it was far enough away that they didn't go regularly. As they sat at their assigned table with cocktails and snacks, close enough to make eye contact with the musicians and just about everyone else in the 150-seat venue, Stu realized they should come more often. There wasn't a bad seat in the house. All the seats—from front to back—were the same price. And if you bought tickets early enough, you were going to have VIP placement.

"Oh my God! I can't believe this ticket!" Tiffany practically squealed when she registered the table tents and posters revealing the act. They were seeing some of his favorite musicians. They were seeing one of her favorite musicians. Robyn Hitchcock and the Venus 3. The Venus 3 included Peter Buck of R.E.M. and two regular auxiliary members of R.E.M., Scott McCaughey, and Bill Reiflin.

Stu raised his glass to Tiffany. "So we're basically seeing Robyn Hitchcock and half of R.E.M. at an intimate dinner theater."

Stu and Tiffany sat side by side, dancing in their chairs to the music. Part of the time his hand was on his glass; part of the time it was on her knee. They held hands and clapped hands, sang along and listened attentively, made eye contact and even got to shake hands with Robyn, Peter, Scott, and Bill after the show.

"That was amazing," Tiffany said on the ride home.

"I'm glad it thrilled you as much as it did me," Stu said. His hands vibrated on the steering wheel, and not only from the movement of the rubber to the road.

"I think the best thrills are yet to come," Tiffany said. And as he took her to her Mount Vernon apartment, as he escorted her up for a nightcap, as they kissed passionately in her living room, she made her decision clear to him. Tonight was the night she was ready to take it all the way. She took him by the hand and led him to her bedroom where they would not experience R.E.M. sleep on that night—and yet it was like a dream.

# WAKE-UP TIME

In Vegas, 2020, Stu floated in a dream-pool of his own memories. Was this a hot tub or a whirlpool? He felt like he was spinning. Skip nudged him. "Wake up, man."

Clint's animated belly laugh made the water slosh back and forth. "Leave him be. Let the guy rest." Clint mock sang, "It's his party and he'll fly if he wants to."

Skip worried. "He'll drown if he falls completely asleep. Resting in a tub is one thing, sleeping is another."

Dana's lips smacked loudly against those of another—the other girl in the hot tub, Stu understood, although he didn't open his eyes to look. The sound stopped and Dana chimed in. "Just keep an eye on him. Make sure he's still breathing. He'll be fine." Dana turned back to Charlene.

"I don't know," Skip said. "If he was in bed that'd be one thing. I think we should wake him up."

Lucy purred. She was close enough to Stu that he could feel her breath on him when she spoke. "I can wake him up." He realized that he wasn't feeling bubbles across his leg and thigh—it was her fingertips.

Stu opened his eyes and almost immediately closed them, forgetting it was broad daylight and that they were outside in an Italian-style garden. He had the sensation of falling, staying above water only because Lucy was holding onto his arm.

He opened his eyes again, squinting, and the surroundings spun.

Lucy laughed. "You awake, sleepy-head?"

"Barely," Stu admitted. He wished he wasn't. The hangover hadn't come yet, but he knew that he'd better pop some pain pills before he went to bed or he could count on a doozy in the morning. Or evening. Or whatever. Their clocks were so skewed that he felt like they'd gone on an international trip, the sunlight contradicting the nighttime he felt belonged.

Skip asked, "Are you doing all right, Stu?"

"I think so."

Clint said, "Of course he is. Just look at him! How could he not be doing fine?"

Stu looked around. The spinning had stopped. He still felt drunk, but in a good way once again. The hot tub had relaxed him and probably had done something to hydrate him as well. He took inventory of those around him: Lucy sat close beside him, Clint and Skip, also in the tub. Dana kissed Charlene across the pool. Barb, who had been dangling her feet in the tub, had left. The statue opposite where Barb had been sitting still looked down upon them. The Italian beauty of stone wasn't going anywhere.

Dana pulled contentedly away from Charlene. "I don't know about you, fellas, but I think we should take this inside."

Stu looked over at Lucy, then back to the others. "I'm in agreement."

"Let's walk," Clint said.

They got out of the water and toweled off. Stu allowed Lucy, her lace panties and bra clinging to her, to keep both his and her towel to cover herself; Dana did the same for Charlene.

The six of them walked back inside The Venetian's inner halls, past the inside that looked like an outside with its outdoor square cafes and bridges over gondola-cut canals. They made it to an elevator that they dominated, despite the young man who stood in it with them, who appeared confused, as though not sure whether to try to tag along with their party or try to escape their lure. They exited and marched, albeit with less swagger, more stumbling, and no head-splitting music, back to their luxury suit.

Skip nudged Stu as they walked down the hall. "Hey Stu. I've got a question."

Stu looked into his eyes and only then realized that his friend wanted to ask him something monumental. What did the guy want at a time like this, while they were in the twilight between drunk and hungover, him about to make out with a pretty girl? Did Skip want some love advice, like how to pick up one of his own? A more direct favor, like, to let him have a shot at Lucy? Or was it financial, as in, can I borrow some money because I know my roulette system is going to pay big dividends. Stu was beginning to feel the coming-on of a headache as he tried to figure Skip out. "So ask," Stu said.

Skip did. "Stu, are you sure you know what you're doing?"

"What do you mean?"

"I don't know. I just have the feeling that you're making a big mistake."

Clint scoffed. "Leave the poor guy alone, Skip. He's a big boy. He can make his own decisions and live with his own consequences."

"Yes, he can," Skip said, opening the door to their suite and allowing everyone to enter. "But that's no reason for a friend not to want to help out."

"Point taken," Stu admitted, closing the door behind them. "But what do you mean? What mistake?"

Lucy began to shiver in the air-conditioned interior, standing in wet underwear and towels, her skin still deliciously damp. "Do you mean me?"

"No, no, not that," Skip said. "I mean, about the ceremony this summer. Are you sure you know what you're doing, Stu?"

Stu showed Lucy to the bathroom and told her to help herself to a fresh courtesy robe. Once she left, Dana and Charlene having already retreated to his room, Stu reassured Skip and Clint.

"Look, Skip, I know what I'm doing. Tiffany and I know what we're doing. It'll all work out, you'll see. In a few months, we'll all be together for the big event, and you'll see for yourselves." Stu found the bottle of prescription Tylenol on the counter and popped two of them, offering the bottle to Skip and Clint.

"Nah," Skip said.

"You'd better," Stu said. "Believe me, you don't want to feel what we've got coming to us when we wake up from this."

"You might not, either," Skip said.

"See you in the morning. Or tonight. Or whenever time it is that we wake up." Stu didn't even know what time it was, but the window gave the luster of twilight to the objects below.

# UP IN THE AIR

On the airplane, Stu fought his after-party hangover with another Tylenol 3 washed down with another bottle of water. He didn't think he'd need it, but he kept the motion sickness bag above the fold of the seat pouch, within easy reach, just in case. He looked forward to seeing Tiffany again when he got home, looked forward to telling her about the amazing lost weekend he'd enjoyed with his best friends. His headache had not quite manifested, but it hovered above him like a sneeze he could feel coming on but that would not fully materialize. He took another sip of his water. Drinking on the plane reminded him of his flight with Tiffany, back when they'd visited Lithuania together. It was his first trip abroad, except for that drunken college spring break in Cancun and a long weekend in Montreal with his family as a kid. Lithuania had been his first time to the other side of the world, and it had left an impression on him.

On that flight, with Tiffany, they drank Krupnikas, a Lithuanian honey liquor, and Riga Balsam, a bitter medicinal spirit, and Vanna Tallinn, a sweet liquor with hints of nuts, chocolate, orange peel, and anise. Each drink was delicious in its own way. Each had worked toward the same effect.

Way before that, and way after their first night together the evening of the Robyn Hitchcock and the Venus 3 show at Ram's Head, Stu and Tiffany had returned to the venue for another show. And another. And another. One show that they didn't expect to enjoy as much as they did, but that was recommended by one of Tiffany's colleagues at work, was the James Hunter Six. James played traditional rock-and-roll on guitar, accompanied by a big bass player, drummer, second guitarist, and two saxophones. Their jazzy, bluesy sound spoke to Stu and Tiffany and became the first band they discovered together. Stu and Tiffany walked into the show late—traffic delays—as James was belting out "I don't want to be without you, baby, like before." That was where they came in, and from that point on, they added James Hunter to their list of acts to see when they came to the area.

On the way out of that show, Tiffany and Stu walked leisurely, hand-in-hand, along the street, deciding which bar to enter—deciding whether to dance or barstool or booth it for the next hour or two. As they walked along the busy, bar-lined street, they witnessed an automobile accident. One car hit another, and the second car bumped a bicycle, causing it to skid. The police arrived within minutes and took their reports, scratching out each person's version of the truth. As witnesses, Stu made sure he gave his account to the police woman first, before Tiffany did. That way, when the others were busy, he could get a good look at the wreckage. There had been nothing unusual about the cars, a Chevy and a Honda. But the bicycle … that was something you didn't see often. No one would be riding this bike home tonight. The chain was off, the gears scattered across the side of the road like coins tossed in the pool of a wishing fountain. Stu stooped down and admired the individual pieces. He picked up a few of the gears and pocketed them like change.

Stu hadn't become interested in wreckage and ruins because of his work with insurance. Nor had he become an insurance adjuster and photographer because of his interest in wreckage and ruins. The two were completely unrelated things until they collided and he made the destined association.

He looked to see that Tiffany was finishing up with her account of the accident as she'd interpreted it. Fortunately, nobody, not even the cyclist, appeared to be injured. Only their modes of transportation were hurt. Of course, Stu figured that at least one of these three would later take advantage of the situation and make an exaggerated claim, based on his own experience working at *Wreck of the Hesperus Insurance.*

Time taken more than mood shaken, Tiffany and Stu decided to skip the bar and head to the car. On the drive back to Baltimore, Tiffany asked, "Are you adding those to your metal and glass menagerie?"

"Maybe," Stu said. "Or maybe I'll fashion it into a gift for you."

Tiffany rolled her eyes playfully. "Sure."

Her reaction made Stu think back to his high school sweetheart, Skye, and the cicada husk necklace that he realized had probably made her breaking up with him easier to do.

He focused on the road ahead as he spoke to Tiffany. "One of these days, you know what I'd like to do?"

"Make me a bicycle chain necklace with a hood ornament pendant?"

Stu laughed. "Good idea. But no. I want to pick up one of those old landscape paintings from a garage sale or junk shop. You know, something worthless. Painted well, but more competent than creative?"

"Okay. Not sure I'm thrilled yet."

"I want to get one of those and then incorporate some wreckage into it. Some gears or glass shards or metal shavings."

"Oh, like those posers who violate worthless landscape paintings with aliens and clowns and robots and absurd figures."

"Sort of like that. Only original. I don't think anyone's doing what I propose. At least, not yet."

"So you're turning into an artiste?" Tiffany laughed.

"Only for your favor, Tiffany. Only for you."

He'd said it. He'd meant it. But he'd never done it.

On the plane, now, he realized that he probably never would. He collected the junk, but lacked the motivation to do anything with it. Stu felt as though trying to make a perfect work of art out of the imperfect fragments of situations defeated the purpose of his collection.

The stewardess asked him whether he would like another bottle of water. Based on the concerned expression on her face, he realized he probably looked as queasy as he felt. "Yes," he said. "Thank you." He looked to ensure the bag still remained within view in the seatback pocket, within easy reach.

Moments later, as he sipped his water, he remembered, again, the drinks they'd enjoyed on the way to and from Vilnius. They'd enjoyed their week in Vilnius and had vowed that they'd return to the Baltics one day. Maybe to Riga, Latvia. Maybe to Tallinn, Estonia. Or maybe they would go to Scandinavia—Finland or Sweden or Norway. Stu had no delusions of being a world traveler and figured there was plenty to see in his own country, in his own state, in his own city. But Tiffany wanted more. Stu and Tiffany had said they would return to that part of the world, motivated by their week in Lithuania. But that had been more than a decade ago.

They'd said it. They'd meant it. But they'd never done it. On the plane, now, Stu realized they probably never would.

# BALTIMORE, MARYLAND

## SUMMER 2021

# THE CEREMONY, PART I

Everyone was here, all of the people important in Stu's life as well as some who were friendly but not so important. Tiffany, to be sure. Clint and Amanda. Skip and Leona. Dana and Marlene, the woman he'd been serious with for the past few months. Many of Tiffany's friends and family—distant relatives—were here.

It was strangely refreshing to see people without their COVID-19 masks and face shields. All of their friends had been vaccinated, presumably had their vaccination passports in-pocket to prove it. It was nice to see three-dimensional gatherings in person, rather than only on video screens.

There were people here that he knew, but not really. People he recognized, but didn't fully remember where from. Faces from yearbooks and gatherings that he remembered from high school or college or past jobs or old parties, but didn't truly remember and probably never honestly knew. Faces without names, and names that popped into his head but that he couldn't pin onto a face in the crowd. Some names, once introduced, didn't match the people belonging to them, their faces and names askew, not matching Stu's memory of them. The Rubik's Cube he'd still never had the patience to solve beyond one side, phantoms from yearbooks and drunken parties and smoky gatherings, manifested but deformed. "Hey, *you*, thanks for coming," Stu said more than once during this outdoor gathering.

And then there were the uninvited guests. Even Stu hadn't remembered, hadn't realized, hadn't kept track of the schedule. Brood X was back. The cicadas had reemerged—and were in full force, Baltimore being the region's cicada epicenter—as friends and family gathered in Baltimore's Sherwood Gardens. Tulips and begonias and trees from around the country decorated the vast gardens, stone benches and chess boards already attracting some of the guests in need of distraction. The rose-twined canopy of black metal stood in front of a hundred unfolded metal chairs, balloons hovering above the floral arch. Portable toilets in plastic blue, reminiscent of old-fashioned telephone booths, lined the park in a far corner. Many of the guests had arrived and cheerfully conversed. Others seemed skeptical, uneasy, unsure as they stared at Tiffany and Stu, more unapprovingly than supportively.

Dana had set up his equipment on a plastic folding table: twin turntables and large speakers, all processed by his Macbook Pro. He began with some R.E.M., throwing songs like "I Wanted to be Wrong" and "Find the River" and "Everybody Hurts" in the mix.

Stu approached him. "No, no, no! Play stuff that's more upbeat. This is a *happy* occasion."

"Is it really, though?" Dana probed.

"It's a celebration! You're putting us in a melancholy mood."

Dana sighed. "Well, if the shoe fits."

"C'mon, man."

"All right." Dana put on "I Don't Want to be without You Baby" by the James Hunter Six. Stu rolled his eyes and shook his head, but let it ride.

Skip, Leona, Clint, and Amanda stood in a cluster with drinks in hand. They casually motioned Stu over. "You guys enjoying the sunny day?" Stu asked.

"Not as much as Vegas, eh?" Clint jabbed.

Amanda rolled her eyes, annoyed. "Keep Vegas in Vegas." Amanda's eyes moved from Clint to Stu. "This is a great place for a wedding. But I don't know about all *this*."

Stu shrugged. "Same story, different chapter."

Skip had a worried look on his face, an expression that seemed to have become his go-to look these days. "It still just doesn't seem quite right, man."

"It's weird." Amanda's pinched-lip expression dared anyone to disagree with her.

"Trust me," Stu took the bait, "Tiffany and I know what we're doing."

Leona smirked, having lost the worry she used to wear on her face. "Stu, you always did march to the beat of a different drummer."

Clint smirked. "Or danced to a different cicada song."

"I know," Skip said. "Can you believe it? Years ago, you gave me and Leona such a hard time for having an outdoor wedding when the cicadas were going to be out. But now, you're having your shin-dig outside with Brood X just like we did. What gives?"

Stu smiled and gave into a complacency that he wouldn't have considered 17 years ago. "I guess you two had your shit together all along. I mean, look at you guys. You've done all right for yourselves."

Stu could see in the glance Leona exchanged with Skip that they'd immediately regretted bringing this up, that it may have hurt Stu's feelings. But before that subject could be breached, as though called by the pulsating sound of the cicadas screeching in the trees around them, Stu excused himself to talk with some other friends across the field. As he walked, Stu thought back to that 17-year-ago wedding in 2004.

Stu had been Skip's best man. There were about 300 guests at their outdoor wedding in Dumfries, Virginia. It had been a nice wedding, a beautiful service. The shade trees stood alive with the cicada noises that they'd all become accustomed to. The screeching had radiated from the branches, providing an applause so loud that it competed with Dana's music at the outdoor reception that followed in the same location. With all of the people there, all of his friends, it was somehow the cicadas and their uncanny love songs that burrowed into Stu's memory and stayed all these years. If Stu were asked for one word to describe Skip and Leona's wedding, it would be "cicadas."

They had been so loud and all-consuming, in fact, that Stu had almost missed his cue at the end of Dana's remix of Metallica's "And Nothing Else Matters." There weren't many things that Stu had memorized, that he could still remember. The Preamble to the Constitution of the United States. The Pledge of Allegiance. The Gettysburg Address. The Lord's Prayer. And his speech at Skip and Leona's wedding reception.

"Ladies and gentlemen, friends, family, and guests." All eyes had come his way, making him uneasy. "Now's the part where I say something nice for the lovely couple." With the insects cheering him on, Stu remembered looking at the newlyweds, remembered how they looked like the plastic ones on the top of their cake, happier than a pair of cicadas newly emerged from the earth. "We have a lot of guests here from all over the country. But if you listen, you'll hear that there are quite a few uninvited guests, too." Stu had paused to let the song of the cicadas illustrate the point.

That's when Skip and Leona began to look a little uncomfortable. They wiggled in their chairs, concerned that Stu might ruin their day. But he didn't.

"Seventeen years ago, I came to Virginia for the first time. That's when I met Skip. And we've been the best of friends ever since. The cicadas were out then. Now, with their return, I've returned to Virginia to visit Skip and share in his celebration of love with Leona." Stu, now in 2021, could still remember the uneasy feeling he'd had in 2004, the unnatural, saccharine taste those words had left as they came from his mouth. He'd strained to mean what he said, had wanted to believe that such true-love fairy tale happiness could be true for someone, if not for him. He had looked Skip and then Leona straight in the eyes and said, "I hope that seventeen years from now, when the cicadas sing their love songs again, I have the chance to return and visit the two of you, still happy, still together, and still in love."

Stu remembered the speech now that he was reciting it in his head. But now was the first time he realized that what he had skeptically wished for them had come true. Here he was, here the cicadas were, and there, just across the green, were Skip and Leona, laughing together at a joke or story Clint was animatedly telling, even Amanda smirking as she shook her head and rolled her eyes. What had Clint said in Vegas? "Even if you can't be happily married, at least you can be married." Looking at his two high school friends and their long-term partners, he saw what Clint had meant right before him, in the flesh. Skip and Leona had always been somewhat child-like, and still looked thrilled to be in one another's presence. Clint and Amanda, not so much—but they still looked like old friends who belonged together, loyalty and love having outweighed passion and romance, but having anchored them together just the same. Being happily married or contentedly married … either one was a perfectly respectable option.

But that didn't mean they were the only options.

The audience in 2004 had appreciated Stu's toast. They'd heartily drunk to it with flutes of champagne. But one can enjoy a good fairy tale without actually believing in magic beans or geese-lain golden eggs. Even having delivered the speech that Skip and Leona had wanted to hear, Stu had wondered about the newlyweds. After their honeymoon, after their early days of discovering one another, after their romance faded into mundane affection, and then into dor-mant co-existence, would they remain happy? That's what Stu had wondered then. When the cicadas of 2004 fell dead, would their marital bliss do the same?

Well, if their present 2021 happiness was any indica-tion—and it was—Stu had been wrong to question the pos-sibility, had been wrong to doubt Skip and Leona's devotion to one another. And it seemed that everyone but Stu real-ized that back in 2004. During the reception, Amanda had advised Leona and Skip exactly the opposite of what Stu had been thinking. "It changes, romantic love," Amanda had said. "It gets deeper, more meaningful."

They had been as sure in their convictions as Stu had been in his. And they'd even wanted to help Stu come around. "Now we just have to do something about Stu," Clint had said with a buddy punch.

"Me? I can take care of myself."

"Sure," Leona had said, the first time Stu could remember seeing the bride of Skip as her own person with her own personality and opinion. "But there's someone out there who can take care of you better than you can. It's just a matter of time."

"Right," Amanda had agreed, seeming to realize for the first time that she and Skip's new bride could be friends and not just wives of friends. "After all, Stu, you can't live like that forever."

Now, lost in thought, Stu forgot who he'd left his friends to go say hello to. Dana dropped "All That She Wants" by Ace of Base, prompting Tiffany to walk directly to Dana. "Really?"

Dana smiled gracefully. "Hey, if the shoe fits."

"You're bad," Tiffany said.

Stu came to join her. "You doing okay?"

"Sure," Tiffany said. "How about you?"

Skip approached, that worried look back on his face. "Should you both be here? I mean, together? Aren't you, like, not supposed to see each other until the ceremony begins?"

Tiffany and Stu both laughed out loud. "Believe me," Tiffany said, "I done seen that, and he done seen this."

Dana nearly scratched his record. "Oh, snap!"

Milton had arrived, wearing a black sports jacket over a white, collarless button down and gray pants. He was the agnostic minister, ordained in the Unitarian Church, who was going to preside over the ceremony. He stepped up to the mic and addressed the socializing crowd. "Ladies and gentlemen, welcome to this … event. We'll be getting started soon. In about …" he referred to his wristwatch. "Fifteen minutes."

Some people nodded and continued their conversations. Others began to make their ways to the chairs arranged before the ceremonial arch. Stu began to feel an uncomfortable stirring in his gut. Fifteen minutes was just enough time. He walked to the far corner of Sherwood Gardens and entered one of the plastic toilet stalls.

# VILNIUS, LITHUANIA

SPRING 2009

# THE WORLD THROUGH AMBER-TINTED GLASSES

It was so crowded in the little pretend bathroom that Stu could barely turn around. When he flushed, the sucking sound of air gave the impression of an implosion. He imagined the waste falling through the sky, maybe hitting a bird with a history of violating city statues in some form of poetic justice. But Stu knew the waste was probably contained in a tank to be disposed of after the flight was grounded. He washed his hands as best he could, pressing one faucet down while the other hand got wet, soaped, rinsed. He opened the folding door, finding two people waiting outside, and brushed past them, returning to the airplane's aisle.

Had Tiffany not waived at him, he probably would have passed her by, zoned out by their long airplane ride and the little bottles of honey liquor, Riga Balsam, and Tallinn Vanna they'd consumed.

"This is so exciting," Tiffany crooned. "Who goes to Lithuania?"

"We do," Stu said, although he was wondering the same thing. Why Vilnius? Stu had never been across the pond and likely would have chosen London or Glasgow or Dublin, Paris or Berlin or Barcelona, Lisbon or Rome or Venice. But that's one thing he loved about Tiffany: her off-the-beaten-path curiosity, wanting to do things usual enough to be comfortable but unusual enough to be, well, extraordinary. She didn't exemplify the wreckage-collecting weirdness to which he aspired, but her desire to visit a more obscure country—one that some of his friends had never even heard of—instead of a mainstream tourist destination—somewhere you could hit with a visit to Disney's Epcot Center—was appealing to Stu.

Tiffany had rented a freshly renovated flat in a 17th century building. The exterior itself appeared like something out of the middle ages, with griffins and angels etched in the stone. Inside, the elevator looked true to the Victorian era, operating with weights and gears and levers. As Stu and Tiffany took the elevator up, Stu peeked through the cracks in the box and watched the inner-workings, fantasizing about coming home one afternoon to find the elevator broken, the parts scattered and ready for retrieval. Antique elevator gears would be a nice addition to his collection.

Inside, the apartment looked like the cover of a brochure targeting the New Russian rich—gold fixtures and faucets, white marble counters and floors, gold and platinum trim on the crystal chandeliers, all the comfort of the Hilton with twice the luxury. And yet, Tiffany assured him, it was half the price of the New York Hilton she'd stayed at during a conference the previous year. A real value. And, most importantly, they were walking distance to Cathedral Square, from which just about all of Vilnius's offerings could be easily navigated by foot.

Going abroad at a relatively young age, Stu had come to realize, could have a meaningful and lasting effect on a person. A drunken spring break in Cancun, Mexico during college and a long weekend in Montreal with his parents didn't really count. A week in another country on the other side of the world as a young adult left an impression—and revealed how very different other cultures are around the world, and how very alike people can be.

Their week in Lithuania was, of course, an eager, hungry week of love and lust, spending long hours exploring the city's sights and long hours exploring one another in their luxury flat. Looking back from his 50s to that time, Stu understood that Lithuania had opened his eyes to cultures beyond his own. He considered it a defining moment. No, America wasn't geographically the center of the world. America wasn't innately right with all other nations a little wrong. Yes, it was possible to watch a newscast about the conflicts and hardships and triumphs of people in the world that was not focused primarily on blowhard politicians and celebrity babies and breakups. And no, Budweiser was not the King of Beers, only a new world regent with a commandeered name at best.

Of course, the thing Stu would remember most about Vilnius was spending all of his time there with the woman he loved.

"Since we're not having a big-church wedding," Tiffany had suggested, "Let's visit all of the big churches here."

"There's no shortage of them," Stu observed, able to see the steeple, dome, or cross of three churches at the same time from just about any point in the city.

They could actually see Cathedral Square from the hallway window of their apartment building, the enormous Vilnius Cathedral calling to them. Stu and Tiffany heeded the call and strolled to the cathedral. White and massive, the front of the cathedral reminded Tiffany of the Pantheon in Rome, she told Stu, which she had seen in family photos but never in person, which Stu had seen in movies like *Roman Holiday* but never in real-life pictures or real life. Vilnius Cathedral's wide, triangular top filled with stucco figures, held up by six massive columns, statues of evangelists looking down from the façade at the classical portico entrance—it all welcomed them. Inside, Stu imagined this to be the type of place a king or prince, queen or princess would marry in, not the likes of him.

The Church of St. Anne, from the front, looked like a scene from a movie: elaborate Gothic red brick, the front façade so welcoming that Napoleon's soldiers found their way there for shelter on the way to Moscow.

"Holy Mother of God," Tiffany said out loud as they looked upon the fairy-tale appearance of the Russian Orthodox Church of the same name. Tiffany led Stu inside to admire a relic that she thought he'd want to see: an icon brought to the church by Tsar Alexander II. "I thought you'd appreciate a relic like this, since you like old things."

"Wow," Stu said as he read the description, "I know Alexander II."

Tiffany laughed. "Sure you do."

"No," Stu explained. "When I lived in York, I went on a city walking tour of old buildings, and one of them was an old downtown house. The Smyser-Bair House, it was called.

The place was converted to an inn, and they had, like, poetry readings and music and stuff during the city's First Friday events."

"Sounds like fun."

"Anyway, one of the rooms at this inn, they call it The Amber Room, after the one in Russia."

"The one that used to be in Russia."

"They have the room decorated in this amber-colored wallpaper from another historic mansion, and they have a copy of the novel, *The Amber Room*, on the bedside table. But the reason they call it the Amber Room is because the guy who lived in the house back in the 1800s, Mr. Smyser, I think. He was given a couple of medals from Alexander II in St. Petersburg at a ceremony held in the real Amber Room, before it was dismantled. You know, before the Nazis got there."

Tiffany nodded. "This icon would go well in a room like that."

"Well, sure," Stu said. "I'm sure they would like to get their hands on it. But frankly, it has a better home in a Russian church like this one."

Later, as they passed vendors on the street selling polished amber and orange-hued plastic with bits of amber inside, Stu laughed. "I always thought it would be cool to have a chip of amber from the real Amber Room. A relic."

"Here." Tiffany picked up an authentic amber stone, purchased it from the vender, and gave it to Stu.

"Thanks," Stu said. "Not exactly the same. This was manufactured for people to buy. A chip from the *real* amber room would be a true ruin. You know, part of a historic place."

"I can't help you there," Tiffany said.

"I did get a chip of plaster from that mansion in York. A bit of horsehair plaster that had fallen from the ceiling in their Amber Room. Close enough."

"So in your mind, a hunk of plaster from an old house is more worthy of a place in your collection than a piece of authentic amber from the Baltic Sea?" Tiffany didn't say "you're crazy," but she wore it in her expression.

"It's not the item itself. It's the story behind it. The item's history." Stu's explanation did not ease her expression.

Stu and Tiffany took an urban hike through non-touristy parts of the city and made it to the giant Church of Saints Peter and Paul, exploring the 2,000-plus stucco figures of angels and demons, characters from the Bible, and historical scenes rendered in Baroque fashion. Closer to home, near Town Hall Square, they attended an organ and choir concert in the crowned Church of St. Casimir. The angelic choir sounded as good as any concert they'd heard on the streets and in the squares of Baltimore, and they found it funny that such spiritual music was being performed in a church that had served as the museum of atheism during Soviet occupation.

Beyond the Church of St. Casimir, they passed through the Baroque Basilian Gate, bright yellow like the sun, and beyond it to the Gates of Dawn, where they followed genuine pilgrims up the stairs to catch a glimpse of the silver-covered Virgin Mary icon. The pilgrims knelt in front of Mary's icon, their heads bowed.

Deep in the cool underground passages of the Artillery Bastion, dating back to the early 1600s, Stu spotted an inch-wide chunk of brick that had fallen away from the wall. It begged to be picked up from the gritty dirt floor. Looking carefully around him, he squatted, as though admiring the wall, and reached down to retrieve the stray fragment. He managed to slide it into his pocket without anyone seeing. Safely outside, as they walked from Town Hall Square toward Vilnius University, Stu showed it off to Tiffany. "This'll be the oldest piece in my collection."

"It's a chip of brick," Tiffany said, squinting in the sun. She looked at Stu, and understood. "A chip off the old block?"

"This little relic, the fortress it came from, is older than our nation. It's really something special." Stu placed it back in his pocket.

Tiffany had a Lithuanian friend in med school who had visited America for a semester as an exchange student from Vilnius University, so Tiffany insisted on a tour of the oldest university campus in Eastern Europe. Her friend, Dalia, was now practicing medicine in Stockholm, so she wasn't able to meet them. But Dalia had recommended highlights of the university for them to see.

Stu and Tiffany checked out the university's courtyards and library, the chamber of muses and hall of writers, murals and statues and brass doors and frescoes. They stopped in the University's Littera bookstore, basking in the colorfully painted interior. Once they removed their eyes from the frescos, they browsed the merchandise and purchased some souvenir postcards. Pictures of the university library doors with their swirly stick handles, the churches and gates and palaces. These scrapbook pictures were better than any pictures they could take themselves. That didn't stop Stu from taking pictures.

The tour of the KGB Museum and prison was more fun than it should have been, given the grim visits to torture chambers and execution rooms. The prison cells included areas of torture, chambers with walls too close for sitting and ceilings too low for standing where prisoners were forced into painful positions for hours and days. The execution hall was brought to life with relics and a video that attempted the perspective of a prisoner's final moments.

On their walk from the dreary KGB prison back to redeeming Cathedral Square, Stu and Tiffany were a little surprised to find a monument to Frank Zappa—the California rocker—right in a square that had once been home to a similar monument to Vladimir Lenin.

"Was Zappa born in Lithuania?" Tiffany asked.

"No," Stu said. "He was born in Baltimore, believe it or not." Signage explained that this Zappa monument had been test as much as testament, a trial commission to see whether newly freed Lithuania was really free to erect a monument to an American rock star, a symbol of freedom to the newly freed Lithuanians. The sign explained that the sculptor, known for creating busts of notable Communist leaders, was contracted to create this rendition of Frank Zappa. This was the first non-Soviet statue to go up in the former Soviet republics after the Soviet Union went down.

"Freedom is something to celebrate," Tiffany said, looking up at Zappa's wavy hair.

"Yes, it is," Stu agreed, finding it somewhat ironic that she would say such a thing given her knowledge of his own lifelong commitment to remaining free, given their recent decision to give that freedom up for one another.

# WATER UNDER THE BRIDGE

Water trickling beneath him, the woman he'd fallen in love with seated at his side, Stu couldn't think of a place on earth he'd rather be than right here, right now. They sat over the Vilnia River, which divided Uzupis from Vilnius. They sat hanging from the bridge above them that connected the Uzupis and Vilnius. The porch-swing hung from two chains connected to the bridge above, and their feet brushed the river's water as they swayed back and forth in this neutral waterway between two nations.

Uzupis became Stu's favorite place during their time in Lithuania, with the exception of spending time alone with Tiffany in their apartment. The "behind the river" community was smack-dab in the center of Lithuania, just across the river from Old Town Vilnius. But in 1997, shortly after Lithuania brushed the Soviet Union dirt off her feet, Uzupis declared her independence from Lithuania. The citizens of Uzupis had their own president, their own congress, and their own constitution. The Uzupis Constitution, displayed on a wall in multiple language, included phrases like "Everyone has the right to live by the River Vilnele, and the River Vilnele has the right to flow by everyone," "everyone has the right to make mistakes," "to be unique," "to love," "to be happy," "to be unhappy," "to understand," "to understand nothing."

"In a nutshell," Stu summed up, "Everyone has a right to be."

In the center of town, Stu and Tiffany got their passports stamped—their real passports—with a Republic of Uzupis seal. Urban art decorated everywhere the eye could see in the small city-state. Eyes and faces made into the bricks of walls. Murals and statues here, there, and everywhere. Graffiti art on the walls depicted porcupines and foxes and mice at laptops and with headphones and smoking pipes.

Backpacking Jesus, arms outstretched in a symbol of welcome, a heavy pack on his back, welcomed backpackers and tourists alike. Mermaid statues peeked out from nooks and crannies along the walls surrounding the river.

Stu and Tiffany made merry in the riverside beer hall where the Uzupis congress met, one rule being that no government decisions could be made without beer. There, at the makeshift beer hall of congress, Stu and Tiffany heard stories of decisions that had been made, dating all the way back to the choice to declare their independence on April Fools' Day—or Independence Day, as it was known in the Republic of Uzupis.

There were small clubs and bars and street musicians to provide background music for their time in this pocket of liberty. Stu and Tiffany enjoyed jazz concerts and blues shows, alt rock and traditional Baltic folk music. They even saw a Frank Zappa impersonator give a performance on the street, his Slavic accent barely noticeable when he sang but thick as kefir when he spoke.

For all of its lovely grittiness, their favorite place in this Bohemian art haven was sitting in the swing above the river, under the bridge, just the two of them. "I could settle down in a place like this," Stu said in a singsong voice.

"Yes," Tiffany agreed. "But in a couple days, it'll be back to reality. Back to work and the daily grind."

Stu nodded. He wasn't sure he agreed. He *could* settle down in a place like this, not just visit it. But he knew that Dr. Tiffany Sher could not.

"Great place for a honeymoon," Tiffany said, nuzzling up with Stu, swinging to and fro.

Stu nodded again, tightening his arm around her. "I'm sure we'll visit a lot of places together. But I have a feeling I'll always think of Vilnius as *our* place."

That's what he had said then, in 2009. That's how Stu had honestly felt. Now, in 2021, he also remembered with clarity what he would later write on one of the postcards they'd purchased at the Littera Bookstore on Vilnius University's campus. Just a year or so ago, he'd taken the postcard with the Uzupis Constitution on the front, and written this note to Tiffany:

> *I'll always love you. I'll always think of you*
> *when I think of Lithuania. But I used to think*
> *of the Gates of Dawn and the swing under the*
> *bridge. Now I think of the KGB museum and*
> *prison. Not to burn bridges, but there's some-*
> *thing to be said for the Uzupis Constitution.*
> *For the right to be free.*

# BALTIMORE, MARYLAND

## SUMMER 2021

# BROODING

Sitting on the toilet in the portable bathroom stall, waiting for the ceremony to begin, Stu mulled over how much had changed between one cicada cycle and the next. How had it come to this? Where had everything gone wrong—or, if not *wrong*, exactly, then how had it gotten him to this place and circumstance?

Stu and Tiffany still loved one another deeply, still cared for each other. Stu knew that Tiffany was his best friend in the world, that she cared for him in a way that only she could—and that feeling was mutual. She confided in him, could talk to him about things she would never bring up with her lifelong girlfriends and sisters, people she'd known thirty years before they hooked up but perhaps didn't know as well because she'd spend more complete and meaningful hours with her one true love than she had with those she loved from the start. Stu understood that their devotion to one another remained unwavering.

Since early adulthood, Stu had always stewed about the longevity of love—or lack of it. Stu had always feared that his cicada cycle theory would prove itself in the real world—in *his* real world. Stu had a notion that romantic love was fleeting even back when Brood X had emerged in 1987, and he was certain of it during the reemergence of 2004.

Then, he'd let his guard down and allowed himself to fall under the influence of his naïve friends and their suburban McMansions. Shortly after 2004, Stu had decided to bury his playboy playbook to pursue the prospect of lasting love. Or at least he opened his mind to allowing lasting love to bloom.

Now, in 2021, the cicadas buzzing all around them reminded Stu of his past convictions. Reminded him that the excitement of getting to know someone offered a higher high than already knowing them all too well. He was ready to return to the way of the cicada.

Stu loved peanut butter and jelly sandwiches. As a kid, he ate them every day. Nothing was better than chunky peanut butter, grape jelly, and wonderful white bread all pressed together. Two sandwiches in his lunchbox, one after school. Sometimes on a Saturday with a bowl of Campbell's bean soup. Or with a baggie of cheese doodles in a packed lunch on a family day trip. When Stu went off to college and started making his own sandwiches, he gravitated to other options after the first month or so. It wasn't that he'd outgrown the selection. It was that you can't eat the same thing every day and expect to continue preferring it. Variety is the seasoning that makes life palatable. Stu valued variety.

Stu had a friend in elementary school who had a copy of *Swamp Thing* on video tape. His friend watched that 1982 movie almost every day for years. By the time they were in middle school, when Stu would come over to do homework and the movie was on in the background, the picture would screech and crinkle, the tape worn thin from so many viewings. Stu, on the other hand, didn't have any movies memorized. If he felt like he was watching a favorite superhero or monster movie too many times, he'd make himself not watch it for a period of time just to make sure he didn't become bored by something he loved. Variety made a fine medicine.

And music. R.E.M. was Stu's favorite band, but other than hearing songs on the radio or in public places, it had been nearly a decade since he'd last listened to an R.E.M. album from start to finish. He'd played those albums to death, too often too quickly, so that now he didn't really enjoy them as much as he believed he should. He knew someday he would return to them like old friends. He would want to listen to them all again. But now he was open to fresh, new sounds to excite his ears. Too much of a good thing was indeed a reality.

Stu knew that Tiffany felt the same way. She had listened to her Robyn Hitchcock albums so often in the early days of their couple-hood that she'd gotten tired of listening to her favorite music. She still enjoyed a live show when he came to town, but she hadn't put on one of his albums in years.

More recently, Stu and Tiffany had begun looking for new acts, going to concerts for artists they'd only recently discovered: Bic Runga and Gaby Moreno, Diego Garcia and the James Hunter Six. Hell, they'd even gone to a Taylor Swift concert recently in an attempt to get in touch with a contemporary pop star who wrote her own songs.

It wasn't only Stu's cold-hearted theory, his brooding over Brood X. Tiffany wanted to disengage, too. She *loved* him, but wasn't *in love* with him. They were best friends—and maybe they would even remain best friends with benefits; time would tell. But they no longer seemed soulmates. Or, if they were, their souls needed sabbaticals from one another.

In the plastic stall, Stu put his face in his hands and pushed back the urge to cry. Now was not a time to feel sorry for himself. This was supposed to be a release, a relief, a moment to celebrate freedom. Why, then, did he feel so empty? Like something was so right, but something else was missing?

Over their fifteen years together, each of them had evolved. She now purchased some of the turn-of-the-century Barbizon artists that they once admired only in museums. The Daubigny paintings they had viewed at the Walters Museum and the Baltimore Museum of Art and the Lithuanian Museum of Art (on loan at the time from the art museum in nearby Riga, Latvia) were not even as nice as the Daubigny she had managed to score at a Freeman's auction in Philadelphia two years ago. It hung as the center of attention in the living room of their shared Pinehurst home, surrounded by an H.C. Delpy and an H.J. Delpy, father and son.

Stu's own collection had expanded to fill three of the four finished basement rooms of their stand-alone house, shelves from ceiling to floor and more shelves and curio cabinets at the center of the basement rooms. Stu called it his "museum of wrecks and ruins." Tiffany called it "his obsession."

Hood ornaments from every type of car imaginable, engine parts, bits of wreckage that only he could appreciate. Volcanic rock from Mount Vesuvius, some found on site by a co-worker who had gone on an Italian vacation, a matching stone found in Pompeii itself. Chips of mud brick from ruins in Arizona and New Mexico. Charred timber and rusty nails and twisted metal from shelled rowhouses and factory buildings in Baltimore and DC and New York City.

The fourth room in the basement? His photography equipment, an ever-growing hobby with ever-increasing expenses. Tiffany complained that his hobbies now cost more than his income, given that he'd never aspired to move beyond his position as a claims adjuster for *Wreck of the Hesperus Insurance*. And he freely admitted that he *didn't* aspire to become a manager or to move to a larger company where there was more room to grow because it was more important for him to be doing what he enjoyed, what was important to him: visiting crash sites for a living and photographing them not just for claims, but for himself.

"People are always defining themselves by their jobs, by how they make money," Stu had more than once griped to Tiffany. "That's only one facet of a person's life, and why should it always be the most important? I define myself by what I love and what I value. My friends and family. My collection and photography. You."

Tiffany, meanwhile, had chased that Yankee Dollar, had moved from a position at Mercy Hospital to a position at an OB/GYN office in Towson, and had moved beyond that to her own partnership with two other prenatal and OB/GYN doctors in Timonium.

In their 30s, when they had first met and fallen in love, he'd been happy to have a mate who didn't want kids, a woman who was afraid to have them given all the complications she saw as a doctor who specialized in complicated pregnancies. But having hit the big 5-0, he regretted that they hadn't had kids, that they would never have kids or grandkids. And right or wrong, he had spent the last seven years letting her know that he regretted it.

Love remained present between them, was there more than ever, woven into the very fabric of their lives. But the excitement was not in their love anymore. The excitement was in their fights and disagreements and discontents. They couldn't even agree on *Downton Abbey* or *Arrested Development*, Amazon Prime or Netflix, Pepsi and vodka or Coke and bourbon, less filling or tastes great.

These petty disagreements came to seem less petty during the pandemic that had them quarantined together for much of 2020 and into 2021. When their arguments came as beginnings or ends to a normal work day and during weekends together, they were manageable. But when their irritation with one another became a part of their daily lives—every single day—the weight of their discontent had become unbearable.

Stu stood from the toilet of the portable restroom and washed his hands as best he could, holding down one faucet and wetting, soaping, rinsing one hand, then the other. The cicadas were giving him a headache with their incessant buzzing and screeching and fingernails-on-the-chalkboard annoyance. He took a deep breath.

The ceremony was about to begin.

# THE CEREMONY, PART 2

Milton, the agnostic Unitarian minister, stood beneath the flowered metal arch in his black and white attire. He announced that the time had come for the ceremony to begin. Stu and Tiffany took their places at the front of the audience, their backs to the people, facing Milton.

There was no maid of dishonor and no worst man. Nobody walked Tiffany down the aisle or stood by to take her back.

Stu was giving her away, and she, him.

Everyone in the audience was aware of what was going to happen. They all knew the deal, understood why they were here. But many of them still looked confused as they watched it unfold, squirming uncomfortably in their seats as though they had cicadas crawling up their skirts or pant legs.

"Ladies and gentlemen," Milton began in a voice that sounded more reverend than befit him. "Friends and family, neighbors and curious passers-by. Dearly beloved cicadas ...."

Some of the members of the audience chuckled.

"We're gathered here today for this non-traditional celebration of love. This ceremonial declaration of independence. We're here to bear witness as this couple, already united in marriage and in love, pronounce their profound love for one another with the act of setting one another free." He paused for a moment, as though conjuring a deep thought from beyond his own personal memory. "As the singer, songwriter, and philosopher Sting once proclaimed: If you love somebody, set them free. Free, free. Set them free."

There was a bit of muffled laughter, a soft muttering beneath the buzz of insects.

"Now," Milton said, "Stu, Tiffany, please deliver your vows to one another."

Stu went first, taking Tiffany's left hand in his. "Tiffany, with the taking of this ring, I, thee, release." He slid the wedding band and engagement ring from her finger. "I've loved you dearly for these last fifteen years of marriage, I loved you before we were married, and I'll love you after we're divorced. What we've forged together during our years of marriage will never die as long as we remain devoted friends. I will always love you, so I set you free." Stu placed her rings in his front pocket.

Next, Tiffany took Stu's hand. "Stuart, with the taking of your ring, I release you." She didn't bother with the formal old-speak, but pulled his wedding band off just the same. "You've been my soulmate and my other half for so long, I can't imagine what life will be like without you. But I won't have to imagine it, because we'll still be the best of friends. This isn't the ending of our relationship, but the beginning of a new chapter for us." She placed his ring in her pocket.

"Tiffany, Stuart." Milton held his hands above them as though blessing them with all his God-given agnostic powers. "With the power vested in me, I now pronounce you divorced and individually free. Although you'll still need to file divorce papers and work out any details not already resolved, like who keeps the house, who gets what, etc. Anyway, Stuart, you may try to kiss the free woman if she wants you to, or not, if you don't want to. It really is up to you. Up to both of you."

Stu and Tiffany looked at each other, laughed, and decided to peck each other quickly on the lips before turning to face their invited guests. Milton said, "Everyone, I give to you Tiffany Sher and Stuart Miller. Just like before, only now… available!"

Dana didn't need to fill the silence following the ceremony since there wasn't any; the cicadas hummed throughout the ceremony and they would reverberate throughout the reception. But Dana decided to take over anyway, hitting the crowd with "Strange Days" by the Doors and beginning the after-ceremony reception.

Stu and Tiffany remained together for the moments after the ceremony ended and before the reception kicked off, that twilight of space that was neither one nor the other, or somehow both at the same time. Tiffany's professional friend, Dr. Hutchens, introduced them to "the guy I was telling you about," Dr. Kendall Mitchell, a single who had just graduated from Hopkins. He looked like he was just *entering* college, Stu thought, this ripped young man appearing more like a "Ken Doll" than a "Kendall."

Stu spotted one of his newer friends, who he'd invited but didn't see earlier; she must have come when he was in the portable toilet. He motioned her over to the cluster of friends and family around them, now including Clint, Amanda, Skip, Leona, Tiffany's sister, Eleanor, and two of her childhood friends.

"Hi, Yolonda, you made it." Stu introduced her to his friends. She was ten years younger, an attractive Latina in a black dress that seemed too formal for this informal occasion.

Dana came on over the mic. "Ladies and gentlemen, if the former couple would join together for the first dance?"

Clint yelled out, "Don't you mean last dance?"

The warble of laughter was barely detectable beneath the drone of cicadas. Then, Dana drowned those noises out. He dropped the needle and the words blared out: "I've had the time of my life, no I never felt this way before."

"Dirty Dancing?" Tiffany asked Stu as they held one another and danced, others watching with confusion.

"I didn't give him any instructions," Stu admitted. "But I did expect him to use a little bit of tact."

"Whatever," she said. "I guess he's keeping it light."

Without attempting any of the film's dance moves as they may have considered doing during their actual wedding reception a decade and a half ago, Stu and Tiffany danced civilly. Midway through the song, they let each other go, taking on new dance partners. They danced with their friends, one-on-one, and with larger groups of friends in circles. Before long, Tiffany was dancing with Kendall and Stu was dancing with Yolonda.

Stu found Ken Doll to be annoying, but he tried to put the perfectly plastic man out of his mind and to focus on his own new prospect. Staying focused on the person right in front of him helped him to not focus on his broken marriage or broken relationship with Tiffany. As she danced, Yolonda smiled at him.

Yolonda was from Mexico City, and she was as hot now as her hometown got during summer. Stu had met her on the job. She had just suffered her first wreck, slamming her Pontiac into the side of a Chevy at a busy intersection. She lived in his old neighborhood on the east side of Baltimore, on Joplin Street in Bayview, and Stu came with his camera to photograph the damage to her car. The red fender was cracked, the bumper bumping the ground, the grill crushed to reveal what was underneath without needing to lift the hood. When Yolonda came out to meet him in her own red skirt and blouse, teardrop pearl earrings bobbing from her ears like side mirrors, he'd wanted to focus his camera on her.

During that visit, she'd invited him in to her rented home for a cup of Mexican coffee—she'd brought it over the border by hand—with cinnamon.

"This is good," he'd said, feeling embarrassingly like a bad actor in an old commercial. "Full-bodied."

She'd smiled at his awkward compliment. She'd explained that she wasn't familiar with how the whole insurance thing worked in this country, asked him to help her understand the process. He promised to stay in close contact with her, to explain every step along the way.

Yolonda had been thrilled when Stu let her know that she would be getting not only enough money to pay for the repairs to her car, but also a little something for signing a form that acknowledged she was not hurt and would not be pursuing medical expenses. He was able to issue a payment of $2,000 for signing the waiver, and she was grateful. "Now that I have all of this money, maybe I can take you out for dinner," she had said.

"Well," Stu had stalled. "I'd really love that. But let's wait until my divorce goes through. In fact, why don't you come to our ceremony?"

"Eh? A divorce ceremony?"

"Yes. In a couple weeks, at Sherwood Gardens. It's beautiful there. We can spend some time together at the reception. And maybe after."

It had seemed like a good idea at the time, looking into her large eyes, imagining having a rebound friend to lean on and show off during the ceremony, to help show everyone that he and Tiffany were both going to be fine.

"A divorce ceremony?" She laughed. "We don't have anything like that in Mexico."

"Most people would say the same thing about here."

Now, at the ceremony, with the cicadas buzzing noisily all around them, Clint and Skip danced with Amanda and Leona, Tiffany danced with her Ken Doll, Dana danced with Marlene behind his dee-jay setup, and Stu danced enthusiastically with Yolonda. For a brief moment, Stu found himself stewing at Ken Doll's hand on Tiffany's waist, shuddered at the reality that he had given away his wife. Had he been alone right now, he would have considered having a good cry. But he made himself focus on the ruins remaining in the wake of his wrecked marriage. Yolonda's half smile drew him in, caused him to refocus on her, and she brushed her hair from her face, looked down to her dancing feet, and then bobbed her eyes back up to meet his. Her sultry smile grew until it was a flirty laugh.

*This* was the noisy romance at the start that he remembered. This was the beginning of another beautifully short-lived passion.

# YOLONDA IN THE MORNING, LONELY IN THE EVENING

The cicadas screeched incessantly. On his side, facing the center of the bed with his eyes closed to the sun-kissed windows behind him, Stu folded the pillow around the back of his head and pressed it into his ears like muffs on an ice-cold day. It seemed an ice-cold day, his first nearly two decades without Tiffany at his side. Freedom was to be revered; loneliness, reviled. He felt the bed cave in slightly, then lift, and remembered that he wasn't alone. He opened his eyes slightly, wide enough to see Yolonda slipping into one of his T-shirts and padding quietly out of his room.

Stu wasn't quite hungover, but he was dangling just under a hangover, the headache not quite there but hovering just above his head like a crown of thorns not yet affixed. He stretched and moaned, listening to hear the sounds of Yolonda getting to know his kitchenette. He allowed himself to smile. The evening with Yolonda had been just what he needed to take his mind off the ruins of his wrecked marriage. Had he been alone now, he would probably be wailing in his pillow.

Yesterday's ceremony had been a celebration, a fitting end to his marriage with Tiffany, a farewell to his intimate involvement with a societal institution he didn't entirely believe in.

He loved Tiffany, no doubt. But why had he succumbed to the impossible prospect of staying excitedly infatuated with the same person—the same flavor of soup or album of music or streaming television series—for the rest of his life? When he allowed rational thinking to reign over raw emotion, Stu was glad that he and Tiffany had given each other the freedom to fulfill their own individual pursuits of happiness.

After the ceremony, it was time for his friends—the guests—to scatter. Clint and Amanda returned to Cincinnati on a red-eye. Skip and Leona had hit the road for a night drive to their home in Charlottesville, where they managed an ice cream shop catering to the students and faculty of University of Virginia, a school they'd once aspired to attend but never seized the opportunity. And Dana was likely hitting the road about now, driving back to Chicago, where he'd landed his dream job as a house deejay for a dance club. Much as Dana tried to stay up on the music of the day, now in his 50s, he ran the dance club's 80s and 90s lounges. Which decade he deejayed depended on the night of the week, but most of the younger club-goers didn't see much distinction between the two. Oldies were oldies.

"Oldies?" Clint had argued during one of their picnic table card games about two years earlier. "Oldies are songs from the 1950s. Not from our lifetimes."

Dana had laughed, peering over a pair of circular sunglasses—and a pair of aces. "It's all a matter of perspective, my friend. 80s and 90s music to you is what 50s and 60s music was to your pops. To these kids today? 50s, 60s, 70s, 80s, 90s—all oldies. First decade of this century will be filed away as oldies before too long. Each its own sub-genre of oldies. But oldies."

Skip folded. "Like us."

"Speak for yourself," Stu pushed the idea away like an overcooked steak. "We've got about as much music ahead of us as behind us. A lot of life to take by the horns. We're only halfway there."

"Yeah," Clint scoffed, "living on a prayer."

There were a lot of reasons Stu had been comfortable with ending his marriage with Tiffany. His lifelong philosophy since high school—since his painful breakup with Skye—had been to not become too attached to one person, to allow himself to exist free and open to any experiences that might come his way. Tiffany had just been so perfect that he was willing—and excited—to make a commitment. Even when he did, he felt as though it were a challenge to his belief system, knowing all too well that "till death do us part" was likely a lie. Even when Stu married Tiffany, he didn't' really believe it would last forever—nothing in this world really did. Their eventual break-up was inevitable. But Stu couldn't help but think that their oldies music conversation had helped give him the push he needed to put philosophy into action. He would be an oldie soon, there was only so much life left, and he needed to get out there and live it.

Now, after their divorce, Stu was back in a tiny, one-bedroom rowhouse apartment, this time in Federal Hill instead of Bayview, and he was almost embarrassed that he'd brought Yolonda to see how little space his domain encompassed. The space seemed more cramped than cozy—especially after sharing such a nice house uptown with Tiffany for the past decade.

He still had most of his stuff at the house in Cedarcroft. Tiffany was going to keep the Pinehurst Road home and pay him half of the equity they had built up, about $200,000. Once he got that, Stu figured he would buy a simple row-house of his own, probably across the city-county line where prices were a little higher but taxes and utilities were a lot cheaper. Until then, Tiffany had agreed that he could leave his half of their stuff (something that would likely be the subject of some debate) in her house. That meant he could keep his museum of wrecks and ruins in her oversized basement.

Stu's shotgun rowhouse apartment, the second floor of three in an old 1800s rowhouse, with lobbyists above him and lawyers below him, was costing him almost as much as their nice house's mortgage for less space than they had in their basement. But he now lived where the action was, more so here than anywhere he'd lived before, and he could walk to any one of a dozen and a half bars and restaurants in just minutes. He looked forward to being at the center of the action again.

The smell of freshly brewed coffee came his way, and he wondered whether it might be wafting in from a nearby coffee shop. Before he could turn to search for a crack in his window, he saw Yolonda returning to the bedroom with two cups of steaming coffee. "It's not Mexican coffee," she said as she waited for him to sit up and take his cup. "Your Colombian will have to do this morning."

"Good morning," Stu said, grinning as he watched her fold her foot beneath her leg, sitting in bed next to him and sipping her coffee.

"You have a nice ex-wife," Yolonda said. "And nice friends. Now you just need to get a nice place to live in."

Stu laughed. "It's a little small, I know, But it's just a starter. I'll be looking for houses soon."

"I can help you look, if you want," she offered. "I have good taste."

"I know," Stu said, putting his coffee down and giving her a one-armed hug. "You'd have to have good taste to be here with me."

She didn't stay with him for long, not on that Sunday. She was dressed and out the door by 11 a.m., explaining that she had plans: errands to run, groceries to buy, and preparations for the work week ahead. It was about half an hour's drive from his place in Federal Hill to her place on the east side. She reminded him that she owed him dinner (although he felt he was the one who owed her now), suggested they get it one evening in the week ahead, and left his place for her repaired Pontiac. He watched from his window as she drove away in her good-as-new vehicle.

Left alone in his apartment the day after his divorce ceremony, Stu wasn't sure what to do with himself and his idle time. He'd only lived here for a few days and had still been spending part of his time at the Cedarcroft house. Now it didn't feel right going there unless Tiffany extended an invitation, so he wanted to stay here at his new apartment. His place was too constraining, after living in a proper house, and he felt a little claustrophobic. Not even enough room to grab a glass of bourbon and pace the house for a good think. "I'd get dizzy if I tried to pace in this place," he said aloud.

There were a few books he'd been waiting for time to read, but they were all boxed up at Tiffany's. Stu thought about beginning to binge watch a show he'd been putting off because Tiffany didn't want to watch (*The Sopranos* and *Ozark* came to mind). But he squashed the instinct because he couldn't, since he hadn't gotten his own subscription to streaming television or cable yet and could only pick up local stations. He'd packed up several file boxes of his pictures when he brought over a few carloads of his clothes, toiletries, and everyday items. As morning inched toward afternoon, Stu made himself a cup of tea and began flipping through some of his pictures, admiring his depictions of the wrecks and ruins of modern-day Baltimore.

He hadn't spent a quiet day alone in ages, always used to having Tiffany around, and before that, people. He was oddly uncomfortable and at ease at the same time. He sat back, looked out his window at the line of rowhouses across the street, and contemplated what to do for the evening.

The truth was, he really didn't feel like going out. He wasn't in the mood to go on the prowl. Frankly, he was tired. All he really wanted was to curl up and think about his predicament. Oh, he had asked for this as much as Tiffany had—cultivated it more than she had. He had been the one who griped about not having his freedom, complained about being smothered, about not wanting to listen to the same album or eat the same sandwich day in and day out. Now, alone, he felt somehow damaged, broken like so many pieces in his collection. Given these unexpected feelings, he had to ask himself: if his lifelong fear of commitment to one woman grew from a fear of being broken, why had he willfully played a part in breaking up their marriage?

"You break it, you buy it," he said aloud as he paced his way back to his bedroom. Stu slowly peeled his clothing off, down to his boxers. His middle ached, and he had the urge to cry, but his eyes remained dry, as though his tear ducts were malfunctioning. "It's for the best," he said to the dresser mirror, trying to convince himself. He had made his bed. Now it was time to lie awake in it.

# KEN DOLLS AND WRECKAGE

"So, how's Yolonda?" Tiffany asked Stu as they sat across from one another at Artifact Coffee. A month after their divorce ceremony, they still got together at least once a week, determined to remain a part of one another's lives even if they weren't sleeping together.

"She's fine." Stu smirked. "Very fine."

"Is your Latina lover enough to keep you at home?"

"We don't live together. I'm still seeing her two or three times a week. Enough, but not too much. And you? How is your Ken Doll holding up?"

"Kendall," Tiffany corrected irritably. "He's a great guy. Smart, funny. I think you'd like him if you gave him a chance. Maybe we should get together, the four of us, sometime. Maybe for dinner or a concert."

"I don't think that would be a good idea." Stu took a sip of his Mexican coffee, just cool enough to taste now. "It's just ... I don't know. Weird, you know?"

"It doesn't have to be. We're all adults."

"Ken does look a little young. Are you sure?"

"I'll bet Kendall is older than Yolo, but who's counting?"

Stu laughed. He actually missed their occasional bickering, how they used to jab themselves playfully under each other's skin as a sort of ongoing game. But as much as he loved Tiffany, Stu had convinced himself over the month since their divorce that they had made the right choice. Sure, they could have enjoyed another few years together. But he just didn't see how anything could last a lifetime.

Yolonda was not in line to become a future wife—Stu was certain of that—but she was fun to be around, and that's the way Stu wanted it. Yolonda had turned him on to new music, Latino music, sounds and rhythms he'd never heard the likes of before and likely never would have paid attention to had they not begun dating. The songs she played for him weren't the Spanish ballads or hits he'd heard before. They had more in common with today's urban pop scene and crooners from the 1950s. He didn't understand what the lyrics were, but he knew the general gist of these songs, about love and lust, men and women, and he knew that they sounded good when he was with Yolonda.

Stu went out with other women, too. Occasionally, he would hit the bars and make his moves on one of the barstool babes. At other times, he would attend the free street concerts and concerts in the square as he had done before he met Tiffany, and he would begin dancing with someone there. Occasionally, Stu would even find a lover on the job. Not usually, but it did happen, a vulnerable woman fresh from an accident asking for his professional help, and wanting to thank him with a drink or dinner after a settlement, sometimes offering more gratuitous gratitude.

Most of these affairs, he understood and they understood, were one- or two- or three-night stands. No strings, no expectations, just fun. That was cool with Stu.

Yolonda was different. She was not one of his one-two-three

girls because she'd already gotten into the twenty-thirty-forty territory. Stu and Yolonda were a de-facto item, even if only unofficially, by the very fact that they continued getting together and making plans to do it again. She was different from Tiffany because he didn't love her—not really, not deeply. He loved being with her, loved her like he loved to have a good time. He cared for her and wished the best for her. But for now, he convinced himself that what was best for Yolonda coincided with what was best for him—simply having a good time together. It was possible to relish visiting an exotic new locale without making any plans to live there.

To fill the void that had once been overflowing with daily love from Tiffany, Stu buried himself in his work. Not so much in *Wreck of the Hesperus Insurance* claims and adjustments, but in his photography and his seeking out wrecks and ruins to plunder and photograph. The two—his job and his work—were intertwined. His insurance claim field work put him smack-dab at the heart of the places he wanted to be: automobile wrecks, house and building fires, ruins of worn buildings or buildings with structural defaults that had, more or less, defaulted. These were all a fertile ground for honing his skills at capturing the dilapidated and damaged on film, and for scooping up treasures of for his collection: charred bits of brick and stone, melted and twisted furnace and hot water heater hardware, shards of fiberglass and metal, and disabled components from under car hoods. His black and white photography began honing in on the hollowed-out silhouettes of burned out vehicles and broken-down shells of recently beautiful homes.

Yolonda and Stu went to an outdoor concert in Mount Vernon featuring Diego Garcia and liked him enough to then pay for tickets to see him at Ram's Head. They went to a free concert in a DC international cultural center filled almost entirely with Guatemalans and South Americans to see a live show by Gaby Moreno, and loved her enough to pay for tickets to see her again at Ram's Head. But Stu shared *his* musical tastes with Yolonda as well. He took her to see Robyn Hitchcock in DC and an R.E.M. tribute band in Baltimore.

When they weren't attending concerts or frequenting night clubs or spending the night together in her Bayview apartment or his Federal Hill apartment, Yolonda and Stu would go out for dinner, walk through neighborhoods looking for interesting houses—for ideas, not to buy—and take walks in city and county parks, like Patterson Park on the east side, Federal Hill in South Baltimore, Druid Hill on the west side, and Loch Raven Reservoir up north.

In early walks, in their early weeks, the soundtrack of their budding relationship was that of the cicadas buzzing with excitement. But months into Stu's time with Yolonda, the cicadas were dying off. Their husks cluttered the grass in places where they walked. Stu even considered collecting a bag full of the husks, to string them together into a cicada necklace for Yolonda. But he realized that Yolonda was a very different person than Skye, his high school sweetheart, had been—and even Skye had not been very impressed with his idea for a meaningful gift.

"Ay!" Yolonda cried, kicking up her foot and grabbing onto Stu's arm for balance. Yolonda couldn't walk barefoot in the grass as she so loved, because within a few steps she would crush the dried husk of a cicada and yelp out. The lush, green trees around them in Sherwood Gardens clung to leaves that were freckled with brown spots where the moisture of life had been sucked dry by the hungry insects. The trees stood tall and mighty, but blemished, weakened, broken down by too much excitement. Huge blotches of leaves were left dry and without purpose, except that of drifting downward to decay. Somehow, Stu had the sense that he knew how that felt.

Stu's bank account had certainly come close to being sucked dry, his paychecks barely enough to afford his rent, utilities, and groceries, and not quite enough to pay for dinners out, concert tickets, and the things that would help him keep Yolonda's affection. Not that her affection was for sale to the highest bidder, but theirs was a fleeting passion and one that he felt he should pay to maintain. He sold a few of his photographs to a gallery in Hampden to help make ends meet.

"When are you going to be able to pay out my share of the home equity?" Stu asked Tiffany during one of their weekly get-togethers, drinking now-lukewarm coffees at Baltimore Coffee and Tea in Timonium.

"When will you be able to move all of your stuff out of my house?" was Tiffany's testy reply.

"It's kind of a catch-22," Stu said. "I need money to buy somewhere to move the stuff to. Then I can move it out."

"It'll be nice to have the space back," Tiffany admitted. "To finally get to use my basement den. But there's really no rush, I suppose. We'll get to it when we get to it."

"I hope you can get to it soon," Stu said. "It would be nice to own my own home. Renting feels so temporary."

Tiffany shot back the rest of her coffee. "I thought that's how you liked it." She hit him with a cool glare. "Temporary."

# BALTIMORE, MARYLAND

SUMMER 2020

# INFECTED

When the COVID-19 pandemic began, it had been all fun and games, at least for Stu and Tiffany. They relished the opportunity to spend all their time together in their spacious home on Pinehurst. Coronavirus was all anyone talked about on the news or in phone conversations—it dominated talk the way it dominated the economy, the health system, politics, and everything else.

On the plus side, Stu and Tiffany and most of their friends and family were healthy, so even if they contracted the virus they knew they would likely be fine, not much worse off than if they were to get the flu. But as the quarantine dragged on from March to April, April to May, all the way into June and July and autumn, and winter, the novelty of being stuck in the house together had worn thin.

"Did you wash your hands and clean your mask?" she would ask when he came home from a grocery run; "Do you really need to visit your hairdresser in her home?" he would ask after overhearing her on the phone making a non-essential appointment.

Stu spent several hours each day on the computer, processing 20 percent refunds on *Wreck of the Hesperus* auto policies while she used online video conferencing to see patients as best she could. Telehealth had been an emerging movement before COVID, but the pandemic had given it the boost it needed to thrive. She had fewer appointments since many patients were opting to wait until they could get in-person visits, so to fill the empty hours Tiffany's practice partnered with a telehealth company, Capstone Health Network. Subscribers to the telehealth network would be referred to Tiffany and her partners under the Capstone umbrella, allowing her to pick up more telehealth business.

In their spare time, Tiffany read the books she had always been meaning to read and Stu watched the movies he had always been planning to watch. They talked about where they might want to visit after the pandemic was over and travel was allowed again—perhaps a return to Lithuania or a visit to nearby Latvia or Estonia. Maybe a trip to Spain or United Kingdom or Germany. And they looked at digital photos of past travels to National Parks, to Lithuania, and to Chicago. Memories and talk of travel made them feel even more imprisoned in their own home. The spacious house began to feel constraining. They cooked together, ate together, slept together, went on masked neighborhood walks together.

And they began to slowly drive one another crazy.

Every morning and evening, Tiffany would tell Stu about the daily Coronavirus cases in the county, the state, the nation, the world—and the number of corresponding deaths. Every afternoon during lunch he would look up from his smartphone to tell her about the latest news or gossip stories: would the pandemic result in a baby boom, or an increase in divorce rates? Tom Hanks had pulled through just fine, but Nick Cordero had died. And President Trump seemed to jump back and forth from one position to another regarding masks, restrictions, the seriousness of the pandemic, and whether they were fighting to defeat a horrendous foe or waiting for it to just go away on its own. But whatever position of the day he proclaimed, he proclaimed it loudly for everyone in the world to hear.

It got to the point that Stu couldn't go out exploring to pick up new pieces for his collection, so he began to find things right within the dwelling. Like a sliver of the ceramic Japanese mug he dropped when the cup of boiling water washed over the side and burned his hand, or the shard of meteorite that had fallen from the casing of the necklace he had bought Tiffany for Christmas last year. Or a shard from the platter she threw at him after he replayed the new 17-minute Bob Dylan song, "Murder Most Foul," one too many times.

"Isn't one listen enough?" she had asked in a shrill voice.

He responded by putting the 17-minute Neil Young and Crazy Horse song "Ramada Inn" on repeat and she countered by stomping off to her home office and slamming the door. Stu wasn't sure whether she blew her top because she found the music annoying, or because Neil whined on and on about a marriage on the verge of collapse.

Prior to the pandemic, going to the insurance office each and every weekday had been a drag and he'd always looked forward to coming home to Tiffany. But now, in the new normal, staying home together had become a heavy weight to bear, like a chunk of meteorite colliding with the earth. After the first few months of the state-of-emergency shelter-in-place, their own appreciation for one another was dipping south quicker than the economy.

"Enough of that shit," Tiffany yelled about five minutes into the fourth replay of Neil Young's nasal drone over Crazy Horse's jam session. "Is there anything he's ever thought that he hasn't already said?"

Stu appreciated the reference, but decided to correct her. "No, wrong album. That's *Greendale*. This is *Psychedelic Pill*."

"Why do you always play that depressing stuff?"

"Well what about that Pink Floyd you were playing yesterday," Stu threw back.

"That's upbeat compared to this disheartening wailing."

"Upbeat?" Stu scoffed. "*Just another sad old man all alone and dying of cancer?* Real crowd-pleasing material, there."

Tiffany yelled out a laugh. "Sure, if you're aiming to pick the rotten cherries, those are the ones you get. There's also the part about *You know that I care what happens to you and I know that you care for me too.*" Tiffany threw up her hands. "But by all means, focus on the parts that appeal to you."

Stu's response was simply to laugh.

"It's like you love depressing stuff," Tiffany continued. "Pictures of old destroyed buildings and wrecked cars. What's up with that? And watching depressing movies? Can't you ever be satisfied?"

Stu took the bait. "What, like settle? I thought I already had—for you."

Tiffany turned red in the face. "You're sleeping in the basement tonight, with your pile of worthless shit!"

"Wait, I was ... I mean ... I didn't mean that."

"Sure you did. It's just who you are. I'm just another piece in your collection, another notch on your belt. Go ahead, move out and find someone else."

"Maybe I will. This is why I never wanted to get married in the first place." Stu spewed.

"You didn't? Then why the hell did you ask me?"

"Because you wanted me to! You wouldn't have stayed with me if I hadn't. And I wanted to keep us going."

Tiffany sighed, then shook her head. "You're a real piece of work. You know, I thought we were going to last. I mean really last, like growing old together. I should have known better."

"It's this pandemic." Stu hunted for excuses, placing them on an imaginary shelf between them. "Being cooped up in the house for so long, falling into a routine more monotonous than any kind of life we planned or expected. We're falling into predictability because of the pandemic, not because of a tedious life, the way my grandparents did."

Tiffany continued her own train of thought. "God knows I should have seen it coming. Should have seen the signs. It's not like you were secretive about your feelings when we first met, when you used to talk about Clint and Amanda and how stupid they were to get married so young, or about Skip and Leona and how they were too naïve and would never last. Or how Dana had his shit together and knew to keep girls at an arm's length so they wouldn't latch on and get too clingy. Or when you talked about how your grandparents' hum-drum lives were less appealing than your parents' more exuberant divorced lives. It's like you want everything that comes together to fall apart."

Stu plodded through her words with his own. "I mean, it's not like we were on a path to follow in their footsteps. We're not boring people, don't just sit around and watch the wheels go round and round. It's this quarantine that's making the difference. That's what's driving us into monotony and boredom. It's not you, it's not me. It's COVID-19."

Tiffany was thinking more than listening. "Or the way you talked about your first summer love and how she broke your tender little heart. What was her name? Ash? Jade?"

"Skye."

"Oh, yeah, Skye. If it wouldn't work with a high school sweetheart like Skye, how could it possibly work with a mature grown-up?"

The snarky tone in Tiffany's voice bated Stu. "It's making you mean, this pandemic. I said some hateful things, too. We're just stir crazy, that's all. We can't fight with anyone outside these walls, so we're picking fights with each other." Stu stopped himself. It now felt more like he was pleading than defending, his collection of excuses growing like pieces in a collection.

"And why is it only with women? Why do you have this fear of committing to a woman like me, but you aren't afraid you're going to grow bored with your friends, like Clint or Skip or Dana?"

"Because my bond with my friends is different. We don't have to live together. If I had to promise to *have and to hold* my best friends every living day of my life, I'd have some commitment phobia about them, too."

She had reeled him in. "So you admit it," she said, more quietly now. "You're afraid to commit. Even after all these years of marriage. You're still afraid."

Stu reflected. "It's not that I'm afraid of us. I'm afraid we'll fall out of love. Maybe we should do something to stop that from happening."

"Kill a marriage to save it from dying? Makes a lot of sense."

Stu shook his head. "No. Ending things on our own terms instead of relenting to what fate has in store for us."

There was a long silence.

"Look at us," Tiffany said. They both laughed, came together, hugged one another. But it was not a laughing matter, and they both knew it. This was the beginning of the end, the first moment in the last chapter of their marriage. The pandemic was still on and they would remain under the same roof until after quarantine released them. Even as they calmed one another, loved one another, the inevitable had revealed itself like an unseen contagion that you nevertheless could tell was there.

# BALTIMORE, MARYLAND

## SUMMER 2022

# FOLLOWING BROOD X

A year had passed since the 2021 tour of Brood X fizzled out. The cicadas passed on and left their offspring deep beneath the ground to wait in monotony for seventeen years. Tiffany still dated Kendall, although they hadn't gotten much more serious, seeing one another two or three times a week. Stu continued to party with Yolonda, although they seemed to have become even less serious about fostering any meaningful relationship, as far as Stu was concerned. He began to feel as though the flashy, exhilarating playboy life he had wanted to resume was not nearly as flashy or stimulating in his fifties as he'd remembered it to be in in his twenties.

The cicadas were dead. And now, in the summer of 2022, so was one of his best friends, Clint. It happened in Cincinnati, in the morning, while most people were going to work or getting their morning coffee. Clint was staggering the streets of Over the Rhine, obscenely drunk.

When Stu got the phone call, it was already afternoon. He was on assignment, visiting a man whose Audi A6 had been sideswiped by a drunk driver. The mirror was knocked off, crushed on the ground beside the vehicle. The slate-painted metal on the front and back doors and been rubbed metallic silver and black, the front and back fenders as well, on the driver's side. The car had been parked on the street in the Rodgers Forge neighborhood, not more than a stone's throw from Tiffany's home, where Stu's museum of wrecks and ruins was still housed. Stu was taking pictures of the damaged Audi, had planned to pick up the broken mirror and swing by Tiffany's to add it to his collection, was listening to the owner of the Audi complain about drunk drivers on these narrow streets, cars parked on both sides of the one-lane Rodgers Forge roads, magnets for accidents waiting to happen for sober drivers, nearly guaranteed for drivers under the influence. Stu's cell phone rang, and he saw that it was Amanda.

Amanda never called Stu—she occasionally talked with him when Clint called or during visits, but that was it. Stu knew it couldn't be the best news. But he didn't expect it to be the worst.

"St-st-stu!" Amanda could barely get out his one-syllable name. "Clint's ... Clint's ..."

"Calm down, Amanda. What is it?"

"Clint's ... he's dead."

"Amanda, no. What's wrong. Is he in the hospital? Did you call 911?"

Stu could hear Amanda crying at the other end of the line. It took her only a moment to collect her emotions enough to respond. "He's dead, Stu. Funeral's Saturday."

"What? What happened?"

"The bastard drank himself to death."

Stu excused himself from the insurance customer and sped over to Cedarcroft, but, of course, Tiffany wasn't home. He called her, but she was with a patient suffering a complicated twin-to-twin transfusion syndrome case. He left a message for her to call him as soon as she was available, stressed that it was an emergency, that there'd been a death in the family.

*In the family.* Stu had said it without thinking about it, but it was certainly the case. Clint was family as much as anyone was. Stu had told Amanda that he would notify Skip and Dana, which he did while waiting for Tiffany to call back. Stu was back home in his Federal Hill apartment, packing a weekend bag, when Tiffany finally called back. Stu told her the news.

"Oh my God, Stu. I can't believe it. What was he, 52, 53? Of course, I'm coming with you. I'll have my assistant call this afternoon and get us tickets together. Does tomorrow work for you?"

Stu hadn't even asked her, hadn't even considered whether he was supposed to ask her, but without a doubt she would be the person he would want to come with him. He let Yolonda know that he would be going out of town for a funeral over the weekend and had to break their date. Yolonda offered her condolences and her understanding. In the hours between finding out and flying out, Stu found out more from Amanda, Clint's mother, and mutual friends.

At the same time that Stu was waking up in Baltimore earlier that morning, Clint was staggering away from a park bench in Cincinnati. As Stu brewed his coffee at home, Clint tripped over a crack in the cement at a city crosswalk and broke his nose. As Stu drove to work in the heavy Baltimore traffic, Clint walked into the heavy traffic of downtown Cincinnati. As Stu processed his first insurance claim of the day, Clint, on a city sidewalk, breathed his last breath and fell forward, his heart stopped, his life draining away.

Clint and Amanda had fought the night before about a meaningless trifle. Amanda barely even remembered what it was—whether or not they could afford to get a new car or whether to trade in theirs for a new one or keep theirs and get a used one—something relatively trivial. But Stu knew well that oftentimes the most heated arguments could formulate around the most unimportant trivialities. Thus, Clint, already a few IPAs in, had stormed out the door, screeched out of their driveway, and headed into the city to blow off some steam at the bar.

Stu was no drinker of virgin martinis, but there could be no question that Clint had him beat when it came to the heavyweight drinking championships. Amanda explained that Clint had been drinking heavily in recent months, even by Clint's standards. It was no longer "tying one on" that was the occasional exception. Not tying one on had become the new once-in-a-while. Clint drank heavily every evening, from the moment he got home from work into the late hours of the night, waking up so drunk that he didn't feel his hangover until he was already at work and a few hours into his shift. Binge drinking had become his way of life. Sometimes, Amanda explained too late, Clint would lash out angrily, sometimes cry pitifully, about how he'd ruined his life by getting her pregnant; how he'd had a shot at a football scholarship if he had only stayed in school; how he'd followed her to live in Ohio when all of his friends lived in different places; and how he didn't have any brothers—any really close friends—where they'd lived the past 20 years. He never declared that he hated her or his family, but he certainly implied that he was not satisfied with his life.

It wasn't suicide, exactly. Clint hadn't intended to end his life. But he certainly didn't do much to save it. In retrospect, Amanda told Stu, Tiffany, Skip, and Leona after the funeral, Clint fit the demographic perfectly. Post-funeral, they sat at the kitchen table in Amanda and Clint's house in Milford, Ohio. Their adult son, Chase, now 33, sat with them but—true to his character—didn't do much talking. Their other two adult children didn't make it, one studying abroad in college and the other abroad in the military. Amanda continued to explain that, as she learned too late, most people who died from alcohol poisoning were white men between 35 and 64, most were habitual binge drinkers who drank five or more drinks in one sitting—you could double that for Clint—and most had a long history of drinking. There was no denying that Clint had crossed the line from casual drinker who tied one on at bachelor parties and celebrations, to living the daily life of an alcoholic.

Amanda looked at Chase with her wet eyes. Age-wise, her son was nearly in that target demographic himself. "So be careful not to make the mistakes he did!"

"I won't, Ma." Chase looked down at his folded hands, keeping the tears in with a tight, stern face. "Never cared for much more than a light beer now and then. Don't think I'll even touch the light stuff now."

Skip cried. "I'm so sorry, Amanda. That we weren't here for him when he needed us."

"Yeah," Stu nodded. "I guess we can't pretend we had no idea that he drank a lot. But I had no clue that it was this serious. He could always hold his liquor."

"Until he couldn't," Amanda said. "If it wasn't this, if he had survived his pity binge, he still wouldn't have kicked the habit unless he went into rehab. And you know Clint. He would have been too stubbornly in denial to do that."

"You don't know that for sure," Stu said.

Tiffany put her hand on Amanda's. "This isn't your fault." She looked around at Clint's son and friends. "This isn't anyone's fault."

Amanda looked down at Tiffany's hand on hers. "It was *his* fault. Clint's fault. Eventually, in a few years, he would have died of liver disease anyway." Amanda blew her nose.

They sat quietly. Stu wanted to say, "You don't know that for sure, you never know," but stopped himself, realizing that it would have been of no help. Stu wanted to say "Maybe if we'd realized it was so serious, maybe if we hadn't partied so much when we were together," but what would that have meant? "If you'd only told us, we could have come; if you'd only let us know, we could have had an intervention," but what would that have implied? Stu sat quietly, knowing that similar thoughts must have been spiraling around in the heads of his friends—and especially Amanda—too.

The room was silent where they sat together for the moments that followed, but none of them was experiencing quiet calmness. The thoughts troubling them individually were buried within, more disturbing than the shifting of tectonic plates—unseen but violent

The following morning, Stu and Tiffany would fly back to BWI. Skip and Leona were going to stay at Amanda's for another two days, and Chase was staying with his mom for a few weeks. Amanda had a network of friends and family nearby and in the neighborhood—as a medical professional, Tiffany stressed how vital that was for her—and Amanda assured her that this network would check on her regularly, and that if a day went by that they didn't, she would either call on one of them or call her.

As they sat at the breakfast table, Stu caught Amanda watching him watching Tiffany. Amanda read his look and laughed. It was the first laugh Amanda had allowed during their visit, and even the laugh was laced with sad sarcasm. But she had something sincere to say.

Stu was afraid to ask. "What?" Had Clint left some weird last request? That Stu was to marry Amanda like a devout brother of biblical times? Or wear his former best friend's class ring from high school, or his worn-at-the-elbows letterman jacket?

Amanda looked at Stu and Tiffany and smiled. "There was this Woody Allen movie a few years back. I guess it was during one of the casting days that Woody realized he was too old to play the romantic lead himself, so he got that ... what's his name ... Larry Bird? Larry Davis? The Seinfeld guy."

"Larry David," Stu said.

"Got Larry David to play it," Amanda continued. "Anyway, in this movie—I didn't care for it but Clint loved it. I'm not a fan of an old creep who marries his own adopted child any more than I'm a fan of an old-looking creep who talks about his hangnail problems at someone's funeral, but that's not the point. The point is the gist of the movie: that life is fleeting. We're all lucky to meet the people we meet and to find the love that we find and the moments of happiness we're granted, and that if there's ever any opportunity for love and happiness, take it. A fling in the back seat of a car, a man, a woman, a weirdo, a normal person, your soulmate or your settle-mate—whatever works for you."

Stu nodded. "You had that—love and happiness—with Clint."

"Sure," Amanda said. "It was in the mix. But that's not what I meant. I mean you two. Who do you think you're fooling? Look at you." Amanda looked at Leona and Skip and asked for corroboration. "Look at them. Am I right?"

Skip nodded. "I always thought their weird divorce ceremony was a mistake. They make a good couple."

Amanda motioned toward Skip. "You see? You guys belong together and everyone knows it except you."

Tiffany and Stu looked at each other and laughed dismissively. "We're still in each other's lives," Tiffany said with a sigh that sounded more content than bored.

Stu agreed. "We do love each other, as much now as the day we met. And as much as the day we divorced. But we know what we're doing."

Tiffany nodded reflectively. "This arrangement works well for us now."

# REMNANTS

Stu found himself prowling Baltimore's darkened inner harbor at two in the morning on July 5. Yolanda's mother was visiting from Mexico City and they were spending time together, mother and daughter. Tiffany had gone out to enjoy the Fourth of July festivities with Kendall. Stu had considered calling up another girl to spend the holiday with, but decided he would rather spend some time in the crowded masses alone. Thus, he went to Baltimore's big fireworks show in the Inner Harbor by himself.

Music blared and fireworks exploded in the sky above him as he stood and watched from atop Federal Hill. He had been to the show in years past and it was always crowded, but it seemed especially populated now, probably because the show—like just about everything else—had been cancelled the year before due to the Coronavirus pandemic. Or because moderate crowds seemed enormous now after a year and a half of partial capacity. Now, most people had been vaccinated except for those who didn't believe it was necessary. It felt perfectly safe to be in a crowd again, at last. The loud music and bright fireworks drew everyone's attention. To Stu, the spectacle was nearly hypnotic.

Anticipation of the aftermath of the show was what had really drawn Stu out at a time when he could have nearly as easily remained home in his Federal Hill apartment with a movie like *Born on the Fourth of July* or a binge watch of *Band of Brothers*. With most of the crowd dispersed, and those remaining now stumbling from one bar or pub to another, the streets were virtually empty of revelers now. Camera around his neck, Stu hunted.

He found remarkable beauty in the aftermath of the firework display. Thin, wide sheets of black ash from the fireworks scattered on the brick, on the concrete, in the grass, draped across overflowing trash cans like melting clocks from a Salvador Dali painting. Stu snapped shots of these bits of ash—remnants of the good time everyone had experienced during the firework display hours earlier.

A thirtysomething couple watched him taking pictures of the ash-draped trash can and stumbled his way, arm in arm.

"What's the idea?" the man asked. "Why are you taking pictures of garbage, man?"

"Because it's beautiful in its own way," Stu answered.

"Are you nuts?" the girl asked—she sounded like she was attempting to sound ditzy. "The fireworks were beautiful. This is trash."

Stu looked her in the eyes. They were bloodshot. "Sure, anyone can appreciate the fireworks—that was the center of everyone's attention. The fireworks dazzled, everyone loved them. People ate their snacks and drank their beers and sodas. They consumed it all and had a beautiful time."

"Got that right, buddy," the man said with a laugh.

Stu continued. "But that was just the surface, the tip of the iceberg. Underneath it all—the foundation that allowed it all to happen—can be seen here. There was the part that everyone saw, and then there's this part that only a few notice, the charred remnants of ash and garbage that allowed it to happen. This is the inside, the heart, the soul of what we saw on the surface."

The man stumbled as he pointed a finger at Stu. "So, like, I want to eat a big, juicy steak, you think I ought to admire my shit the next day?"

The woman wrinkled her nose. "Don't be gross."

Stu knew these jokers wouldn't understand. But *he* understood. This mattered.

"Here, look." He turned on the photo display on the back of his digital Nikon and showed off some of his photographs from the evening. Singled out, focused upon, seen out of the context of the world around them, the spotlight on the items alone, these pictures of things most people would subconsciously overlook actually appeared alluring. The ash, seasoned. The bottles and cans and wrappers emerging like a mountain from the green-striped garbage cans, pleasant. As Stu looked at the pictures himself, even he seemed a little surprised when he focused on them. He looked up to register the same enlightened expressions on these two strangers' faces—if in part because they were under the influence.

"Wow, not bad," the man said. "I'll never look at garbage the same way."

"Say!" the woman snapped her fingers. "You're like those picture takers who took pictures of ugly things, like those starving women in the depression and bombed buildings in World War II, or homeless people on the streets. You take ugly things and make them look good."

Stu cracked a smile. "They're already good. Photographers just try to show them for what they are, warts and all. Everything doesn't have to be photoshopped picture-perfect. There's beauty—or relevance—in everything. Even the things people don't want to look at."

They got to the most recent picture on his camera—the one of the trash can with trash and ash. The three of them looked at the picture, then at the real deal in front of them, then back at the picture. True, the photographer played a role in making it look more presentable, not just in pointing a finger at the subject. It looked better in Stu's photo: the metal stripes of the receptacle had more sheen, the ash had a richer texture, even the bottles and cans and wrappers glistened in the light of the photo's flash.

"That's good stuff," the man said, smiling.

"Yeah," the woman said. "You should put your pictures in a museum."

Stu laughed. "Like a museum of garbage? And wrecks and ruins."

"No, really," the man said. "I thought you were a freak when I saw you taking pictures of filth. But I gotta hand it to you, that's good stuff."

The woman nodded. "Let's go get a drink."

Stu shook his head. "Nah. Thanks but no thanks. I want to get some more shots before the cleaning crew starts eliminating the evidence."

"Keep up the good work," the man said.

"See ya." the woman giggled, and the two walked off to another club.

Stu exhaled a soft laugh. He'd always known it, but somehow this drunken couple at two a.m. in Baltimore's Inner Harbor validated it for him: his work mattered. His collection, his photography, his unique perspective on these ugly underbellies—wrecks, ruins, and the castaway leftovers that others ignored—it all mattered. Before this encounter, he had been ready to call it a night, to stroll leisurely back to his little rowhouse apartment. But now he felt a new vigor to capture more while it was here.

The result was more than just a collection of about three dozen spectacular photos intermixed within the few hundred that he took. The result was—to his surprise—a dozen framed photographs on display in a show at the Creative Alliance in the Patterson Theater, seven of which sold. More validation that his collection and his work mattered.

# STILL LOOKING AFTER ALL THESE YEARS

Before the Fourth of July, a couple weeks earlier, Yolonda had found someone else to go with her to the Kanye West concert while Stu was in Ohio for Clint's funeral. That was just as well, as far as Stu was concerned, not really being a fan of someone who would publicly say that was a "proud non-reader of books" and that he "would never want a book's autograph." Stu wasn't beyond being self-absorbed himself, his examination of his own life and relationships sometimes quite wordy. The more words he searched to examine his feelings for Yolonda, the more he realized that he just wasn't that into her.

Stu had allowed feelings to develop with his Latina lover, but he felt strangely unconcerned that she had so easily found another date on such short notice—as unconcerned as he was that he didn't get to watch the rapper—is that what Kanye West was, a rapper, or a singer, or an artist?—in a live show.

Stu made it up to Yolonda by getting tickets to Panteon Rococo, a Mexican band from Monterrey—the one south of the border—who had a show coming up in DC. He knew she was a sucker for Latino music, and although it wasn't his cup of tequila, he enjoyed being there with her, watching her dance to the reggae, punk, and salsa-spiked music, dancing along at her side. After the concert, less than a week after July 4 and a few weeks after Stu had returned from Clint's funeral in Cincinnati, they went to Yolonda's rented rowhouse in Bayview. Yolonda made them drinks and put on something more comfortable that looked so tight that it couldn't possibly have really been more comfortable. She allowed her bubbly personality of the night to fizzle out, and sat beside Stu on her small leatherette sofa. "I'm sorry about your friend."

Stu sighed. "Me too. But, weirdly, it's not as big a surprise as it should have been. Not in hindsight. He was only 52. But still, he still drank like he was 25 and still crashing frat parties." Stu took a sip of the margarita she had given him, half a pitcher frosted in a plastic blender carafe on the rectangular table before them. "He was the first to marry, the first to have a child. But he never really grew up."

A concerned look covered Yolonda's face. "From what you described," she said, beginning to massage his tense shoulders, "Clint drank a lot more than we do. And a lot more often. You can party, my friend, but you can't party like that."

Stu looked into Yolonda's deep brown eyes and realized that he really liked this woman. But he didn't love her. Tiffany's deep blue eyes contained so much more complexity. Yolonda's eyes reminded him of a Paul Simon song from decades ago. They reminded him of cold coffee.

But her coffee-and-cream body was hot, and she used it to help relax him, to help him take his mind off his lingering sadness. He was glad to have Yolonda with him to shoulder through this rut. He was satisfied.

It turned out, Yolonda revealed over hot Mexican coffee the next morning, that the Kanye West concert she had attended with Jamal had been one of her favorites, that she'd really enjoyed the show and the date had gone well. Stu didn't ask *how* well the date had gone after the show was over, but he could imagine. Probably just as well as some of his one-two-three date encounters had gone. One out of three of them, for Stu, could have replaced Yolonda if Yolonda were to become unavailable. As the second half of his second cup of coffee cooled, he realized what he'd really known all along: that although he and Yolonda were infatuated with one another, although they knew and enjoyed the curves and contours of one another's bodies and minds, they were simply fulfilling the emotional and physical needs of one another for the moment, not progressing toward any kind of long-lasting relationship. Stu sighed. "Whatever works," Amanda had said, referring to the Woody Allen-Larry David movie as well as Stu's current situation with Tiffany. And *this* was working for now. But Stu knew that this was not what Amanda had meant.

Refilling his half-empty cup, ever-mindful of the need to keep things hot, to keep things flowing, Yolonda laid another surprise on him. "Too bad you couldn't see Yeezy with me. You got me make-up concert tickets to Panteon Rococo, Stu, and I got you some make-up tickets, too!"

"To who?" Stu momentarily ascended his melancholy mood with a smile.

"U2's Three-Sixty III tour at the American football stadium!"

"U2 at M&T? That should be a great show!" Stu got up to hug Yolonda. It was being referred to unofficially as the "spin around three times" tour because it was the third rendition of the "three-sixty degrees" tour. Although Stu felt the band had never really topped *Joshua Tree* artistically, he did think that some of their post-Apple iPod spokespeople albums were refreshingly mature and novel at the same time. And some of their recent shows, according to reviews he'd read and clips he'd seen and one of their concerts he'd attended himself about ten years ago, had become spectacles in and of themselves, with high-art designers putting together elaborate sets and laser-light shows.

"Didn't the same designer do the elaborate stages, sets, and effects for both Kanye and U2?" Stu asked, looking at his smart phone to check. "Yeah, Es Devlin's her name. Interesting stuff. Their music may be night and day, but maybe the shows will be more artistically alike than you'd normally expect."

"I knew it would make you happy, Stu!" Yolonda danced in place, almost jumping up and down in tiny leaps of joy.

Stu couldn't help but laugh as he watched her giddiness. "I can't wait, Yolonda!"

They didn't have to wait long. Stu parked nearly an hour's walk away from the M&T Ravens Stadium, knowing that not only would parking be hard to find and expensive, but traffic would be unbearable. He and Yolonda enjoyed walking hand-in-hand, arm-in-arm, through the city streets. City walks were a great way to pump themselves up for a show beforehand and to discuss a show after having experienced it. Stu dressed in an untucked button-down and jeans; Yolonda wore one of her signature tight sweater suits that hugged her figure as completely as he wished he had the capacity to do.

Oftentimes on such walks, they would see an accident or two. During this walk, on the way to the late-afternoon show, they did not. Perhaps traffic was just so congested that there wasn't room for the vehicles to pick up enough momentum for a crash, or maybe everyone was just paying close attention to where they were headed on these streets with so many names. Stu kept his senses alert, a second-nature quality for him, waiting for something to see.

"Would you look at that?" He let go of Yolonda's hand and walked toward a gutter at the corner of a traffic-light intersection. He always found the remains of accidents in places like this, had spotted a few already during this walk, but they were typically the same: plastic headlight and taillight shards, strips of tire rubber, glass pellets from windshields and windows, wiper blades, L-shaped license plate frame fragments. They most commonly came from Chevys and Fords, Toyotas and Hondas, Subarus and Kias and Hyundais. But within this little pile of un-swept remains, he found the cracked, scraped Mastretta shield. "It's a Mexican car."

"From Mexico City," Yolonda nodded. "My home town. I've been to the Mastretta factory, on a school tour." She, too, seemed excited at the find. "You don't see many of those around here."

"I've never seen one around here," Stu confirmed. He could still make out the checkered flag over the green-white-red of the Mexican flag, half rubbed raw from the scrape against asphalt. "This is a keeper."

Yolonda put her arm in his and drew him close, pressing her body against his as they walked on with the damaged shield in his pocket. "Most things from Mexico City are keepers," she said with a ripple in her coffee eyes.

A different vibe radiated from Yolonda on this evening, as they entered the football stadium and climbed the mountainside of bleachers in search of their seat numbers. This was a different sort of venue, not an open square show where you could dance or a dinner-theater setting with seats at a table. In their stadium seating, they barely had room to dance in place, and became even more cautious after watching a hefty, middle-aged woman holding a plastic tumbler of beer slip and fall forward, over the people in the seats in front of her, landing on her back in a shower of suds. The woman was okay—she stood and laughed it off—but it could have ended a lot worse for her. Stu had already been feeling the weight of mortality in the days following Clint's death, so seeing the woman's antics in front of him made him less animated in his dancing at Yolonda's side, more aware of the fragility of life itself.

When Edge's guitar riffed into the beginnings of an extended rendition of one of the band's classics and Bono began singing, "I still haven't found what I'm looking for," Yolonda interlocked her fingers with his, pulling him gently toward her, took his other hand, and looked into his face with a sly, confident, sexy smile of contentedness. She danced in a trance, easily maneuvering her body in a natural sway that came closer and closer until she was touching him in a hundred points of contact. Some 35 years after launching the song, Bono professed that he still hadn't found what he was looking for, but Yolonda seemed to be telling Stu, with her nonverbal cues, that perhaps she had. She seemed to be telling him, "Hold me, thrill me, kiss me, kill me."

After the show, they walked hand-in-hand through the sea of people, beyond the vendors selling knock-off tee-shirts and ball caps, posters and CDs. They took another route to the car, walking through the inner harbor, the moon reflecting off the water of the Patapsco River. When they reached the courtyard next to Scarlett Place condominiums, they stood beside the pedestal that once held up the statue of Christopher Columbus. That statue had been pulled down by protesters in the summer of 2020 and thrown into the harbor, later recovered and reassembled on private land. Standing in the harborside courtyard in what once would have been Columbus's shadow, Yolonda pulled Stu close to her, faced him, and planted a passionate kiss on him. Her teeth gently scraped his lip as she pulled away, looked into his eyes, and said, "I love you."

Stu looked at the colossal brick-red mountain of condominiums beside them, remembering the last time he had passed by the Columbus monument with Tiffany, remnants of red paint still remaining on Columbus's chest from when he had been vandalized by protesters as a sort of foreshadowing to his complete overthrow and relocation. "I've had a wonderful time tonight, Yolonda. You're the best."

She moaned out a contented laugh—more defensive than accusatory—and they continued, hand-in-hand, making their way slowly to the east side. They walked along Eastern Avenue, through Little Italy and past South Broadway, past Fells Point. When they got to the south-west end of Patterson Park, they took a detour into the green expanse, past the pagoda, along the green grass, and they exited near the southeast corner. They passed by the golden-domed Ukrainian Orthodox Church on the right side of Eastern, passed by the Patterson Theater and Creative Alliance—marquee lit up—on the left.

"That's the place that had your pictures?" Yolonda asked.

"Yep, that's one of the places. There, and the Visionary Art Museum."

Yolonda giggled. "You're a famous artist now."

Stu let out a stark laugh. "Not hardly. But maybe I can get my stuff into a small gallery or two now."

They continued walking aimlessly, forgetting what they were looking for—his car—let alone finding it. He'd parked along the street in one of the few areas left with free street parking. He could have just as easily parked at his place in Federal Hill, only they had left from her place in Bayview and planned to return there for the night after the show.

As they continued walking leisurely in a lackluster search for his car, they soon found themselves passing the Southeast Anchor Branch of the Enoch Pratt Free Library. Stu looked up in disbelief.

There, in the courtyard before the library, surrounded by the crisp-brown foliage of relatively young trees, Stu couldn't believe what he saw staring back down at him. A tall, silver pillar towered above them. At the top of the pillar, the familiar bust of Frank Zappa. Dazed, Stu stared, mouth agape.

Yolonda laughed, tugged at Stu's arm, tried to wake him from his reverie. "What's wrong?"

"I've seen this before," Stu said. "In Lithuania. In Vilnius."

"In Vilnius? What were you doing there?"

Stu's expression of astonishment melted into an easy smile. "I was there with Tiffany. On our honeymoon."

"You take Tiffany all the way to Vilnius to see Zappa, and I only get to walk the expanse of Baltimore's inner city," Yolonda joked.

Stu looked at her and laughed. "But it couldn't be the same statue." He looked back up at Zappa's windblown hair. "They wouldn't have moved it here."

"I don't know," Yolanda said, seeming to grow impatient with the head on a pole. "Maybe they didn't want it anymore."

Stu would learn later, curiosity fueling his investigation, that this bronze bust of Frank Zappa was an exact replica of the one still standing in Lithuania's capital, a gesture of good will from the city of Vilnius to the rocker's hometown of Baltimore. A gift.

Stu looked away from Zappa and back at Yolanda, her caramel skin taking on a luxuriant hue in the moonlight. "Well, that was thirteen years ago. Weird." He took Yolanda's hand and started to walk, but she remained anchored next to Zappa.

Yolanda looked back up into Zappa's empty eyes, then into Stu's. "You're still in love with her."

"Tiffany?" Stu scoffed. "Nah. We've always loved each other. But we're not *in* love."

"Sure, Stu. Keep fooling yourself." She looked up at the impaled head as though seeing the inevitable end of their own relationship in those soulless bronze eyes. She looked from Zappa back down to Stu and smiled. "You're as in love as I've ever seen a man."

# FACING THE MUSIC

After the night of the 360 degrees concert, after stumbling onto the Frank Zappa monument in East Baltimore, after Yolonda witnessed Stu's in-the-moment reaction to his memory of honeymooning in Vilnius with Tiffany, Yolonda hadn't warmed his coffee with nearly as much finesse and care as before. Nor did she warm it as often. They still went out—to concerts, to dinner, to his place, to hers—but the frequency slowed from a few times a week to a few times a month. Everything appeared the same on the surface—the quality if not the quantity—but Stu got the hint. She had thought she'd found what she was looking for in him, and all he was looking for was a casual "for the-moment" friend. She had kept him on her hook for the fun they had, but she had abandoned her single line for a net and was fishing in deeper waters now.

He fished too. He prowled and hunted, aimed and attacked. He tried to be a gentleman about it. The waters didn't seem quite as stocked as they once had been at the free concerts and clubs he frequented, so he began using an app on his phone to find new flings. He found that getting the girl ahead of time allowed him to relax and enjoy the music at the shows, not as intently attentive to every fine female face around him.

Some women sounded ideal online, but proved to be less so in person. Others seemed modestly withholding in their profiles, but delighted him once they opened up in person.

Jenny turned out to be one such woman. In her profile, she said that she liked French paintings and French wine, cityscape sunsets and city walks, dance music from the 70s and 80s and the gentle sound of a rippling stream. It sounded a little flaky to Stu, but maybe just what he needed for an ABBA tribute band at Merriweather Post Pavilion.

When he got to know Jenny beyond her bubbly personality, she had some complexity to her, not entirely unlike some of the better ABBA songs. Jenny and Stu took long walks in the city, and she admired buildings like the Bromo Seltzer tower, was able to tell him about how the designer had traveled to Florence, Italy, and visited the Palazzo Vecchio, and modeled this clock tower after it. They went for a hike at Gunpowder Falls Park, and when they got to a remote streamside area, she suggested they stop, find a flat rock to sit on, and meditate. Only the sounds of stream, bird, and the rustling of leaves came to them during those precious, quiet moments.

When they went to the Walters Art Museum, he was surprised when she gravitated toward the Daubigny painting—a sunset on the coast with a horse—and he had the urge to tell her that it was one of Tiffany's favorite artists, that he and Tiffany (or rather, Tiffany) had a Daubigny hanging in the living room.

Short, stacked, and full of energy, a few weeks into their once-a-week dating, Jenny meant almost as much to Stu as Yolonda did, and he saw Jenny even more frequently. Jenny's crystal blue eyes twinkled when she laughed, and she had a way of brushing her long blonde hair off her shoulder that reminded Stu of the way Tiffany did the same thing.

As they listened to the Swedish pop music of ABBA, Jenny's hips swaying next to his, Stu decided to heed the pop advice that spilled from her lips: "Take a chance on me."

When Stu learned that The James Hunter Six was returning to Ram's Head, he waited on his smartphone the day that tickets went on sale, managing to buy two side-by-side seats located one table back from the stage. He'd considered inviting Yolonda, but decided that Jenny would appreciate this music more. She did.

At the show, they danced in their seats as she sipped a French red and he sipped a winter microbrew. As the band broke into "This is Where We Came In," Stu leaned back in his chair, took a mouthful of beer, and began to scan the room at old and young music lovers enjoying the show. Stu imagined that Ram's Head was a place he could continue to fit in even when larger concert venues became coliseums to the young. The folks in the crowd spanned generations, people who looked half his age alongside people who looked (almost) twice his age, all enjoying the music.

Stu contently explored the crowd as he listened to the loud rock and roll. "Baby, I know this show like the back of my hand," James swooned between sax and drum riffs, "and I've got to go for it's more than I can stand ..."

Then, Stu spotted her.

Just a few rows over and one ahead, to the right of the stage, Tiffany sat with her date, her blond hair bouncing as her head bopped, just a sliver of her nose, lips, and eyelashes visible in silhouette from where Stu sat, her back to him. It had to be her, he was sure of it. Without realizing it, he began looking at her more than he looked at the stage, and it didn't take long for him to confirm that it *was* her with complete certainty.

After the show, Stu told Jenny that he'd spotted a friend in the audience, that he wanted to say hello, and he towed Jenny behind as they navigated the rocky sea of people flowing against him. "Hey, Tiffany!"

"Stu?" Tiffany gave him a hug. "What are you doing here?"

"You know I like good music," Stu said. He introduced Jenny.

"And this," Tiffany said, "is Joe. Joe's a counselor at Shepard Pratt."

"Nice to meet you," Joe said. He stood tall, a few inches taller than Stu, and looked like top-brass Army action figure, a bit on the older side. Stu imagined this was what G.I. Joe's father must look like.

"Let's get a drink," Stu suggested. Tiffany agreed, and Joe and Jennifer, somewhat reluctantly, followed their leads.

They got a bar booth in the adjoining restaurant, the loud conversations all around them serving as background music. Stu imagined that Jenny would have preferred to be down the street at the dock in the moonlight with only the sound of trickling water and their kisses to penetrate the perfect stillness. But this was a fine turn of events as far as Stu was concerned.

"A counselor, huh?" Stu probed.

Joe forced a half smile. "I help returning veterans and stateside drone pilots cope. I'm a vet myself, so I bring some authenticity to the therapy table."

"Joe and you share a hobby, too," Tiffany said. "Joe's a photographer."

Jenny chimed in. "I love photography. I mean, art photos, not smartphone selfies."

Joe laughed. "I take pictures of veterans. From WWII to recently back from current conflicts."

Jenny raised an eyebrow. "Oh, that's interesting."

Joe looked down at his beer. "Yeah. I don't know, but there's something in a person's face when they get back from war. They wear some of what they've seen and done on their faces. It's hard to explain, but if you look at the pictures, I think you begin to understand a little." Joe looked at Stu. "What do you take pictures of?"

Stu stalled, deciding how to put it into words so it didn't sound creepy or insignificant, but Tiffany answered for him. "Oh, he shoots wrecks and ruins."

"Like, train wrecks?" Joe had a troubled look on his face, emphasizing his etched, hard wrinkles—the type he probably captured in his photos of vets.

"Once I shot a derailed train," Joe said. "But mostly car accidents. And old building shells."

The word "shells" made Joe flinch.

"He collects the stuff, too," Tiffany said with an affectionate laugh. The mixed drinks she'd been consuming had gotten the better of her, and he could tell she was more relaxed than she may have planned. She spoke freely. "That reminds me. When are you going to move all that junk out of my basement?"

Jenny's face washed over with confusion. "What?"

"Oh, didn't Stu tell you?" Tiffany asked. "We used to live together."

Stu clarified to Jenny. "Tiffany's my ex." It didn't sound right.

Tiffany put her arms in the sign of an x and made a talent-show-judge buzzer sound, then laughed. "We were married, then we had a big break-up bash!"

Joe tried to lighten the subject. "So, Stu, what do you collect, exactly? Old house numbers and license plates? Stuff like that?" It sounded like Joe was putting on his counselor's voice, as though Joe wanted to help him with a mental illness.

"Just ... interesting pieces from what's left after disaster. I mean, I have some volcanic rock from Pompeii, and some chips of stone from the Roman Forum, and the Mayan pyramid of Chichen Itza. Pieces of history, you know?"

"That's cool," Jenny said, seeming to appreciate where this was going.

"But I don't stop there. I'm interested in today, too. So I collect little bits and pieces from modern day disasters. Hood ornaments and twisted metal from auto accidents. Charred brick and rusted nails from old rowhouses and buildings. I have a broken drum stick from the last show before R.E.M.'s drummer quit, and a splinter from one of Babe Ruth's bats."

Joe leaned forward, an empathetic look on his face. "So you gather broken things."

Tiffany said, "Tell them about the house fire across the street from you. How you practically risked your life to go in and scavenge."

"Well, it wasn't that dangerous. Just another burnt-out rowhouse shell," Stu said. But he remembered it well. It was before they were married, when he still lived in his first-floor rowhouse apartment on Elrino Street, in the Bayview neighborhood on Baltimore's east side, the neighborhood where Yolonda lived now. He'd awoken with sweat on his face, smelled smoke, and had the feeling that something was wrong. He sat up, stood out of bed and looked out his window. Flames engulfed the rowhouse across the street. He pulled his clamshell phone from his nightstand and dialed 911.

"Fire! There's a fire on the 300 block of Elrino Street!"

The fire department was right next to their neighborhood, so they made it within minutes. The firefighters hosed down the house, axed through the picture window and door, rescued the one person who was inside. The woman had tried to bleed her own oil tank line, didn't want to pay the $50 to have a professional do it, according to the online report. After the fire was put out, the place was boarded up, condemned, and as far as Stu knew, no one had ever fixed the place up or moved back in.

As the sun set on the day of that fire, Stu had snuck over to the shell. He found the back basement door unlocked and ventured in. The beams of the house looked like wood in a cooled-down fireplace, black and cracked like so many squares of onyx. The old furnace had exploded, pieces of metal all over the ashy basement floor. He picked up the furnace's sliding vent mechanism and held it in his hand. The four little sections still opened and closed as he slid the tab back and forth. Carefully, gingerly, he walked up the basement stairs, into the charcoal-black room of the first floor. There were areas where the floorboards did not feel stable, where his foot sunk down into the bow of the wood planks. He looked around at the burnt papers and books, furniture and knick-knacks. Two matchbox cars on the floor lay half-melted and twisted. He picked them up.

Stu had gone back to his apartment with the items in his hand, had returned under cover of darkness with a shopping bag to collect more bits of charred debris: wood, metal, nails, utensils, the stub of a melted toothbrush, a Randy Savage action figure whose face and one arm had melted, his legs missing.

Now, with Joe's eyes twinkling in anticipation, Stu decided not to describe that night in more detail than Tiffany had already done. "I got some interesting pieces there, from the furnace and the charred beams. It's surprising to see the burnt shell of a rowhouse from the inside, to see how vulnerable even the strongest-looking brick home really is."

Joe nodded. "We're all more vulnerable and needy on the inside than we pretend to be on the outside. We do what we think we have to in order to make it in the world, to fit in. But one thing I've learned is that everyone has the capacity to break. That's why it's important to look out for each other. Especially the ones we love."

Jenny sighed. "That's sweet." Stu could swear she was flirting with the old man.

Joe continued. "You seem very interested in broken things. The things you collect and the photographs you take. Sometimes we confront the things we most fear as a way to prove to ourselves or to others that we can handle the worst the world has to throw at us."

Stu didn't appreciate being psychoanalyzed, so he did his best to turn the tables. "I think you're right. Like a person might deal with their own difficult memories from war by photographing veterans who have seen combat and lived to bear the scars."

Tiffany rolled her eyes for Stu to see. Stu knew Tiffany well enough to realize she was changing the subject to avoid the eruption of a battle at their table. "I'll have to admit, though, that Stu has proven his vision a few times. His pictures have been displayed in museums and theaters."

Jenny looked at Stu with new eyes. "Wow, that's amazing."

Stu shrugged it off.

Joe raised a glass. "Good for you, Stu. It's not the norm for someone with a quirky creative hobby to find an audience who appreciates it."

They all clinked glasses, finished their drinks, and left it at that.

As Stu drove Jenny from Annapolis to Baltimore that evening, it wasn't the James Hunter Six ringing in his head, but a song from the ABBA tribute concert he and Jenny had attended on their first date. Breaking up was never easy, but knowing Jenny, knowing Stu, it was the best they could do.

# SWEEPING UP THE JOKERS

Time continued ticking, faster now, it seemed, than it ever had before. Stu had always heard older people tell him that time went faster the older you got, but he'd always imagined that if he just slowed down to smell the roses he'd be able to slow down the time. It didn't appear to work that way. When he slowed down—when he went *out* less often, hooked *up* with fewer women, took *in* fewer concerts, enjoyed more *down* time by himself—the time went by just as swiftly. It would soon be time to plan the next get-together with the guys. The first one that wouldn't include Clint.

Stu remembered one of those guy-getaways from many years ago, in 2004, back when Skip had found Leona and had made his intention to marry her clear. Skip had characteristically fallen into one of his trite proclamations. The three guys—Stu, Clint, and Skip—had rented a hotel suite with a pool-side patio and spent the weekend going crazy with drinks, conversation, music, and cards. They played poker that night on a table out on the hotel suite patio, under the moonlight, Clint swatting cicadas and making a mess. Stu poured them each a shot of whisky between hands and proposed a toast.

"To women," Stu had proposed.

"No," Skip amended as he raised his own glass "To true love."

"Gimme a break," Clint had said. The three men shot back their drinks.

Skip had finished his shot, but he wasn't done with the subject. "Since meeting Leona, I've learned what true love is." They each fanned out their cards as Skip enlightened the fellowship. "True love is when you love someone so much that you don't need *them* as much as you need them to need you."

Clint spit out a sunflower seed. "True love is a crock of shit. I learned that the hard way." He jabbed Skip with his elbow. "By getting married!" Clint took a swig of beer.

Skip went on the defensive. "Don't you love Amanda? I mean, you bitch a lot about her, but you love her. She was one of the hottest girls in high school. You're lucky."

"Lucky?' Clint thought about it as he studied his cards, growing serious. "Yes, I love her. But it's a different kind of love. It's … I don't know." Clint didn't look comfortable being sincere, unless the nature of his sincerity was anger or aggression. "Just be sure you know what you're doing, Skip. Know for sure that she's the right one, that this is the right time." A hum filled the air when the conversation hit a pause, the cicadas there to fill the empty silences.

Stu remembered thinking—but not saying—during that visit that the cicadas aroused different people during different cycles. They had lit a fire in Clint's heart back in 1987, when he was courting Amanda. In 2004, they were getting Skip all hot and bothered for Leona.

Beyond that, Stu considered that the subject of death, as well as romantic love, followed the cycle of the cicada. It was during the 1987 emergence of Brood X when his grandfather had died. During the 2004 cycle, an uncle had passed away. Stu had contemplated, "whose soul will they sing for next time around, in 2021?" The Cicadas were off by a year, but the answer had been delivered. Clint would not be joining them for another hand of poker.

Clint had, in some ways, been their strongest proponent of playing cards. It had been his idea back in the high school lunchroom. And after they'd all gone their own separate ways and then come back together for hikes and parties and get-togethers every several months, it was often Clint who brought the deck of playing cards and pulled them out when the opportunity presented itself—or forced them in when the opportunity didn't.

"Remember back in high school?" Clint would ask, knowing full well that Skip and Stu couldn't forget because there was no way he would let them. Clint enjoyed reminiscing about the glory days. Stu understood that it was, in part, because those were the best days of Clint's life. Clint had an excited memory of his youth, in part because it was lost prematurely in the webbing of his complicated marriage. When loosened by whiskey and beer, Clint sometimes admitted regrets in the first decade of his marriage: that he wished he'd finished high school and gone to college and not gotten married so young. He'd had a good shot at a football scholarship. He could have been a success, something he didn't feel he was to his own wife and kids.

As Clint's marriage matured and his kids grew up, Clint voiced such regrets less and less often. He fell into his life with his family and began to take more pride in them. He loved them more and more as time passed, and there was no denying, as far as Stu was concerned, that Clint had made some difference in the world. But hadn't everyone who ever lived, from the mightiest king to the littlest cicada? Stu knew that everything had worth and everything mattered; from the burst of a firework to the charred ash that made it possible.

Now, in 2022, Stu had the Leonard Cohen song in his head, reminding him that Clint had not left them very much, not even laughter. Just another tired man who was laying down his hand "like he was giving up the holy game of poker."

Stu wondered whether he and Skip and possibly Dana would give up card playing for their next gathering just because it would remind them of playing cards with Clint. Stu didn't want to play cards anymore. Maybe it was just the mood he was in—Cohen could do that to a person—but Stu was having less fun playing the game. Poker, bachelorhood, nightlife, the whole damned party. Stu was beginning to feel like he wanted to trade the game he knew for shelter.

# ANNAPOLIS, MARYLAND

## SPRING 2023

# OLD FRIENDS

Stu saw less and less of Jenny, and even less still of Yolonda. He stopped checking his dating app messages and stopped looking for fresh squeezes. Maybe it was the Leonard Cohen Boxed Set that he'd downloaded, but he'd been in an introspective and melancholy mood. Stu had more than a wheel stuck in the ditch; he was immersed in an immense pothole. But he felt like this rut was what he needed: a crack for the light to get in.

Since the night that Stu and Jenny had run into Tiffany and Joe at Ram's Head in Annapolis, Stu had been thinking more and more about Tiffany. Before getting rid of his dating apps, he scanned through some of the highlights—and low points—of his romantic adventures of the past couple years.

What he hadn't fully realized as he was getting it on with the selection of the moment was crystal clear now, as he looked at an in-a-flash summary of the women and their qualities. Love of music, interest in art, a desire to help others, and an enjoyment of helping one's self, long walks by day and dance marathons at night, a strong will, an open heart, and patient empathy for the pieces in Stu's unusual collection and the stories behind them ... all of these qualities that he sought in other women were Tiffany's qualities. It had been *her* that he was searching for all along.

At first, coming to an understanding of this, Stu thought about trying to create some elaborate setup, perhaps snaring her with a dating advertisement that he knew she wouldn't be able to resist, or sending her a letter as a secret admirer, or having orchids sent to her with a message that the delicate flowers could thrive if nurtured. But all of these impulses tasted a little too much like Pina Coladas caught in the rain by the dunes of a washed-up cape.

So instead, Stu simply invited Tiffany to a concert. That had, after all, worked about seventeen years prior, after the cicadas had died off years ago, after Skip and Leona's wedding.

Simon and Garfunkel tribute bands were nothing new, and there had been a number of them over the years. But now, with the impersonators getting older themselves, there was a tribute band that was actually performing as the aged Paul and Artie, replicating the Old Friends reunion tour of the early 2000s. The act even got Everly Brothers look alike/ sound alike musicians to do the intermission show.

Tiffany loved the idea, and they went to Ram's Head for the show.

In the car, driving from Baltimore to Annapolis, Stu felt uncharacteristically vulnerable. He cared about the outcome of his actions, didn't feel his usual *what happens will happen* attitude, and that gave him pause. "I miss us," he said, looking forward.

"Me too." Tiffany let out a deep breath, as though she'd been holding it inside her—tucked away in some membrane beneath her ribcage, somewhere close to her heart—for a long time. "I miss us too. You're my best friend."

Stu looked at her and smiled. "I love you."

Tiffany cleared her throat, perhaps stifling a tinge of emotion. "Yeah, that's obvious." She cracked a grin. "I've known that all along."

Stu laughed. He drove with one hand on the wheel, his other hand finding Tiffany's.

At the venue, Stu and Tiffany looked at each other nearly as often as they looked up at the musicians. The music sounded better that way, anyway, the musicians in the mind's eye rather than in the eye of the beholder. The tribute band really sounded like the older Paul and Artie, but they didn't quite look the part when seated this close to the stage. Besides that, the view and the music and everything was better when Stu and Tiffany faced one another and made it a private moment.

"Waiting for the sunset," the Paul-man sang with is old friend.

The Artie-man harmonized in, "Memory brushes the same years ... silently sharing the same fear ..."

On the way out of the venue, a vendor was selling tee-shirts from the original "Old Friends" concert with the real Simon and Garfunkel pictured on them, the tour dates and locations listed on back. Stu bought one for Tiffany. She reluctantly stretched the oversized shirt over her sleeveless yellow blouse.

Back in Baltimore, they decided to hit a club, to go dancing. They parked in Little Italy and walked to Power Plant Live. As they did, Tiffany realized that she couldn't quite live with the T-shirt's giant pictures of two old farts, two balding men bouncing on her breasts. She slipped it off and offered the black concert shirt to a panhandler working a medium at the center of a crosswalk on President Street.

Stu hadn't felt this excited buzz in years—the excitement of romance that had not come as he'd anticipated when going on fourth and fifth and sixth dates with recent women. Tiffany looked radiant, her smile a perpetual laugh, as they danced together in the sweaty crowd.

When Stu took Tiffany to Cedarcroft, to drop her off, she invited him in. Tomorrow's dawn was closer to them now than yesterday's twilight, and they were still abuzz with their decision to give themselves another shot.

"Stay?" she asked, more request than permission.

"Yes," he said, carefully. He pulled himself closer to her, as close as the two of them could stand without becoming one. He knew he was foolish for thinking that. They'd virtually become the same person already, before they got their divorce.

When Stu returned to their family bed, it wasn't a steamy den of decadent pleasure so much as an exciting return to who he loved and who he was. Stu and Tiffany had both had other partners in the years after their divorce. But tonight, for the first time in years, they made love.

The next morning, Stu and Tiffany woke together as they had thousands of times before. But the morning felt fresh and new, Tiffany nuzzled into Stu's chest, sunlight pouring in through the blinds and casting golden stripes across their bodies and across the tangles of sheets between and around them. "Good morning," Tiffany purred.

"Yes," Stu said, and kissed her. "Very good morning."

Tiffany slipped from his arms and sat at the edge of the bed, the sunlight draped over her golden skin. She slipped into some pajamas and kicked into fuzzy slippers. "Coffee?"

"Sure," Stu said, sitting up himself, reaching for his discarded clothes on the bedside floor.

In the breakfast nook of the kitchen, they sat over steaming mugs of Peet's Coffee, contemplating whether to cook up some eggs and sausage or to go to IHOP or Waffle House. They decided to slice up a fruit salad with some yogurt. They would go out for a late crab cake lunch in a few hours.

"You know that postcard from Vilnius?" Stu asked. "The one with the Uzupis Constitution on it?"

"Of course I know it," Tiffany said. "I hate it."

"Can I have it back?"

Tiffany left Stu at the kitchen counter, cutting apples and pears and peaches, while she went to the office to rummage through some papers. She came back with the post card in question. Stu washed his hands from the sticky fruit juice and dried them on a towel hanging from a counter handle. He took the post card from her. On the back, Stu had written, "I'll always love you. I'll always think of you when I think of Lithuania. But I used to think of the Gates of Dawn and the swing under the bridge. Now I think of the KGB museum and the prison underneath. Not to burn bridges, but there's something to be said for the right to be free."

Stu read the words. They stung him now. He looked up at Tiffany. "I've been thinking about Vilnius lately. I've been thinking about the Gates of Dawn and the cathedrals, and the swing over the river."

"Water under the bridge." Tiffany smiled.

Stu nodded. He ripped the postcard in two. "I'm going to take this down to my museum of wrecks and ruins." He started toward the basement door.

"And while you're there," Tiffany called after him, "why don't you dust off our rings?"

# BRYCE CANYON, UTAH

## AUTUMN 2023

# FROM THE BOTTOM LOOKING UP

Down Stu went, his knee nearly buckling at times, trekking poles helping him to keep his balance. Dana walked directly in front of him, leading the way, although no tour guide was really needed since the path was clearly marked. Skip followed behind, taking a drink from his canteen more often than the others, but drinking a little less each time to make it last.

"Is this really worth it?" Skip griped.

"Oh, you just wait until we get to the bottom," Dana hushed him. "Then you tell me."

Stu huffed contently. "It'll be worth it."

So they'd given up the holy game of poker, at least for this get-together, for the fun of a few days exploring the parks and sites of Utah. They hiked in Bryce Canyon National Park, surrounded by hoodoos so top-heavy that they looked like they might come crashing down at any moment, as though one accidental sneeze or tumble could set the entire national park on a domino-like path of destruction. They all knew that appearances could be deceiving, that these thin towers of sandstone with large rocks on top had been standing here for lifetimes, and that, to the hoodoos, the presence of three hiking men was of no more consequence than that of three cicadas buzzing through the green of an outdoor wedding.

At the bottom of the Canyon, they found some smooth pink boulders and sat down. "Would you look at that?" Dana outstretched his hands, inviting them to bask in the glory of the view.

Stu nodded. "And to think, all of this beauty is the result of damaged goods."

Skip laughed. "What a warped way to look at it."

Dana nodded. "Whether it got this way through cultivation and care or depreciation and erosion doesn't matter. The fact is, it got this way, and it's perfect—if perfect is a real thing."

"It's not a real thing," Stu said. "But that's okay."

They sat and looked for some time, basking in the majesty.

Stu thought about Tiffany, who was probably sitting down to dinner about now, the time being later in Baltimore than here in Utah. When they were apart, Stu still caught himself thinking of her before the sudden accident, perpetually surprised and then resolved each time that he did. She was able to walk again with the aid of a cane. He remembered the night of her accident in a series of flashes and scenes, some of them his, some of them seeming to be from his own memory but not possibly so, being that he wasn't with her. He knew his mind was filling in the blanks, providing him with an imagined memory of scenes she had relayed to him.

It had happened about four months ago, in late spring. Tiffany and Stu were asleep when the call came. "Dr. Sher," the receptionist from GBMC—Greater Baltimore Medical Center—had said in a strangely calm voice, "Dr. Hutchens needs you at the hospital. The twins are coming." The twins in question were suffering twin-to-twin transfusion syndrome, a rare condition in which one twin was feeding off another, harming it. In some cases, the weaker twin could die from not getting enough nutrients; in other cases, the stronger twin could die from overeating.

"I'll be right there," Tiffany said to the phone. She turned to Stu. "I've got to go."

She threw on her doctor's attire and jumped in her car, taking Gittings to Charles Street. It was at the intersection of Charles and Dumbarton where a driver ignored the stop sign and jutted out into traffic. Tiffany slammed right into the front driver's side of the Ford Taurus, both vehicles coming to a complete stop. Stunned, each driver remined in place until the ambulance arrived. The medics helped the other driver out of his car and Tiffany out of hers. The other driver got the stretcher and Tiffany got the bench seat. Fortunately, GBMC—where Tiffany was headed anyway—was only a few minutes away.

By the time Tiffany was in the back of the ambulance, she was coming to her senses and realized she couldn't move her right leg. She didn't really feel pain because she was still in shock.

"Oh my God!" She feared that her leg may be paralyzed. She realized later, upon reflection, that the other driver was in worse shape, not even conscious on the stretcher. But in the moment, her concern was for her own wellbeing—and that of the babies she was supposed to be helping.

"I'm a doctor," Tiffany tried to tell the emergency room doctor as she rested restlessly in the hospital bed. "I was on my way here to the delivery ward. I'm supposed to be assisting Dr. Hutchens."

The ER doctor smiled at her. "Don't worry about that right now. I'm sure Dr. Hutchens is managing on his own. We need to take care of you right now."

Stu didn't remember the exact details, but he did remember getting the call from Tiffany the next morning. He had figured she was still at the hospital helping with the patients and was shocked to learn that she was a patient herself, that she had already undergone surgery on her leg, and that she would be in a wheelchair for at least a month before being able to put weight on her right leg again. Stu left his cereal to absorb its milk and rushed to the hospital himself.

In a panic, he found her room and came to her side. She smiled when she saw him. "I'm okay. I'll be fine."

"You should have called me last night, right when it happened! I would have been here."

"I was completely out of it then, when it happened," she said. "And there's nothing you could have done. They took care of everything."

"I could have been here," Stu said. "That's something."

"You are here." Tiffany smiled. "You're here now. That's everything."

Later in the day, Stu sitting at Tiffany's bedside, the doctor came to give them the news. She would be confined to a wheelchair for two, maybe three months. Then, she would be able to walk again, but only with the aid of a cane. It was likely she would need to use a cane for the rest of her life.

"You're very lucky we didn't have to amputate," the doctor said.

Tiffany had been smiling when Stu first came, to assure him she was fine. Now, she did not smile. When the doctor left, Tiffany cried.

"I'll be here for you," Stu said. "I can take some sick leave and stay home to take care of you. Don't worry. You'll have the hang of the wheelchair in a few days, and you'll be back on your feet in a few months."

Tiffany sniffed. "One of the babies. I didn't mention it before. One of the twins died. The smaller one."

"Oh." Stu wasn't sure what to say. "It wasn't your fault that you couldn't make it. And maybe if you were there it wouldn't have made a difference. Maybe it was bound to happen and you would have just been there to see it happen."

"True," Tiffany said. "That's what Dr. Hutchens said when he told me. Probably inevitable. Still, I should have been there to try to help."

"You worry about you," Stu suggested.

"Oh, I'm sure I'll have plenty to worry about in the weeks and months to come."

"I'll be right with you," Stu assured.

Tiffany let a laugh fall out of her mouth. "Guess I'm just like everything else in your collection now. Damaged goods."

Stu shook his head and took her hand. "No, don't say that. You're perfect. Maybe you're more perfect now than you were before. We'll get through this together."

There was more Stu wanted to say as he held her hand at the side of her hospital bed, but he refrained. Stu had not said it—it probably would have been the wrong thing to say—but it did occur to him during those first days and weeks of assisting her around the house, bathing her, helping her onto and off of the toilet, and caring for her, that in a strange way—in a good way—maybe she was right. She was, in a way that he could appreciate, damaged. Maybe, Stu considered, this was the ultimate purpose for his living of a life focused on damaged goods: to cultivate himself into the type of person who not only would love and take care of Tiffany after such a disabling accident, but to be the man who actually found joy and meaning in the act of assisting an injured person.

No, looking around at the hoodoos of Bryce Canyon, knowing that as strong as each might be there was the possibility of any one of them toppling at any given moment, Stu realized it was right that he did not speak such a thought aloud to Tiffany, that it would have sounded more weird than meaningful. But the thought remained with him. Damaged or not, he loved Tiffany and wanted to take care of her—in sickness and in health. Whether she had another car accident or slipped during a hike; whether she got cancer or heart disease or any other of a million ailments, he loved her and wanted to be with her.

As Stu, Skip, and Dana stood in the valley and prepared to ascend the path before them, they looked forward to what awaited them at the top. They looked forward to the rest of this visit together, a visit filled with hiking and sightseeing and conversation and comradery. They looked forward to returning to their own lives in their own homes with their own loves. They all looked forward to Stu and Tiffany's second wedding—yes, they were doing it again—and Stu looked forward to that most of all.

Stu, Skip, and Dana looked forward to the next get-together after that wedding, not sure whether it would be at a blackjack table, a picnic table, a rock in the middle of a canyon, or an elevation marker at the top of a mountain pass. But before taking the first step up out of their present valley, Stu encouraged them all to wait a little longer, take a few deep breaths, and to really examine the view.

The hoodoos surrounded them on all sides, earth red, sandstone white, a rainbow of stone towers like the growing "magic rock" farms from their childhoods. Only these rocks were bigger, natural, massive. Just as the three friends were bigger, their desires natural, their prospects massive. Yes, they looked forward, but now they paused in what seemed a nearly perfect moment to reflect on the present.

Another perfect moment: when Tiffany and Stu decided to get remarried. When he told her what he'd realized in the days before taking her to their own personal reunion concert: that all of the things he'd been looking for in other women were already in one package: her. She agreed that the excitement, the buzz, the feeling of initial romance was back between them—but more importantly, so was their mutual respect and affection, a sense that together they were greater than the entirety of their individual selves.

A few weeks after that Old Friends tribute show, when Stu asked her in bed if she would marry him again, she'd laughed. "I didn't think you were going to ask ... yet."

Stu grinned. "Well, when did you think I was going to ask?"

Tiffany did the math in her head. "Like, in about fifteen years? In 2038, when the cicadas come back."

"Oh, no way," Stu shook his head. "We could never wait that long. I'd be ... sixty-eight years old! You'd be sixty-five.

We'd both be collecting Social Security. I could never wait that long."

Tiffany had agreed, they would have a nice, quiet, outdoor wedding in a neighbor's backyard, just their best friends and family. This time, without the annoying guests—the cicadas—buzzing all around.

"You see?" Tiffany asked later, as they enjoyed brunch at home. "Your theory was bullshit all along. When you're really in love, when you're really excited, you don't need to follow the cycle of a cicada. You follow your own path."

"Our path." Stu nodded. "I've got a few cicada husks on one of the shelves downstairs. I could always bring them to the wedding. Something old? I could fashion them into a necklace or bracelet to go with your wedding gown."

"No need to. I'd say they belong right where they are. On the dusty basement shelf."

Now, in Bryce Canyon, thinking about his upcoming wedding reminded Stu that he had some unfinished business. "Hey, Skip." Stu looked at his friend with eyes that wanted to reveal something big, something as monumental as the landscape around them. "I have something to ask you."

Skip broke away from the scenery and looked at Stu with excited anticipation, as though attempting to figure out what Stu was looking so stoic about. "So, ask."

"Will you be my best man?"

Dana laughed out loud. Skip conjured up a scene from earlier in their friendship, when their roles had been reversed. "If I'm the best man you can find."

Skip had known long ago, he later explained, back before Stu knew, before Stu figured it out and then lost sight of it again and then figured it out again: If you decided to see the negativity and the impossibility in a relationship, you would certainly find both. But if you were willing to filter that away and focus on the possibility and the positivity, that was there in equally ample supply. Not always. Each couple was unique with unique sets of merits and problems. But Skip found it to be true in their situations. For himself and Leona. For Stu and Tiffany.

"Just look at that," Dana said, regarding the towering hoodoos, putting his arms around his buddies. "Sometimes the best view is from the bottom looking up."

Skip and Dana nodded their agreement. After a few more moments, knowing that the sun would begin its descent soon, Skip led the way back up the path, back out of the valley.

Stu noticed a little pointy rock at his feet. He knelt down and lifted it from the dust, brushed it, blew on it, and took a closer look. No more than an inch long, not more than half a centimeter wide at one end and an inch at the other, this appeared to be the tip of one of the hoodoos—an ancient pinpoint from a hundred-foot giant, somehow flicked away by an unseen force of nature, perhaps a natural disaster, and left on the canyon floor to be found by him. A keepsake for his collection if he'd ever seen one.

Just because these surroundings appeared as a perfect view, just because a moment was perfect, didn't mean he needed to try to keep that moment for himself forever. Feeling the ages in his hand, the tip of the stone pressed into his thumb, Stu considered what a fine addition this would be to his shelves. Between the volcanic rock of Mount Vesuvius and stone from the Roman Forum; amidst the Spirit of Ecstasy, his souvenir from Vegas, and the Mastretta shield, his Mexican souvenir; near the melted and deformed WWE action figure and matchbook cars; beside the broken, charred, and damaged bits of metal, glass, and wood.

Then, Stu stopped himself, decided to place the point right back where he found it, right back where it belonged. He took a photograph of the piece. He had been snapping a healthy number of photographs during this visit, envisioning a series of broken, weathered, and worn rock formation photographs to display in a gallery or small museum show, his work having gained some prominence in Baltimore and, to a lesser degree, in the Mid-Atlantic region. His work, his friends, Tiffany—everything seemed to have fallen into its right place. It all mattered.

Stu had noticed it at an early age and he came back to the thought often, pondered it now as he stood in the valley of hoodoos: sometimes, things that normally did not seem to belong together, when forced into close proximity, resulted in collaborations of unique and unexpected beauty. Like the hoodoos all around them, the result of millions of years of damage. Or the collision of two vehicles into a twisted metallic sculpture worthy of inclusion in a museum of modern art. Or his photographs of wrecks and ruins, of burnt out shells, of houses and dilapidated buildings, of trash and ash. Or the friendship between three men who had drifted on lifelines into directions so far apart from one another they likely never would have considered getting to know one another had they met at a social gathering for the first time today. Or like his unexpected reunion with Tiffany.

As Stu followed his old friends up the dusty path, as he thought of Tiffany waiting for him back home, Stu finally understood that there was no reason to worry about being broken or about broken relationships. He and his friends and his work and Tiffany—like the fallen crown of the ancient hoodoo—were all right where they belonged.

THE END

# AUTHOR'S NOTE

In 2005, as I became more involved with Baltimore's literary community, I participated in a new fiction writing workshop co-sponsored by the CityLit Project and the Creative Alliance. I remain friends with several of the budding authors I met in those early *Write Here Write Now* workshops.

Most of the short stories I fed through the workshop were the stories that would become *Tracks: A Novel in Stories* (Atticus Books, 2011). One of those stories was "One Last Hit," published in the *Freshly Squeezed* anthology (Apprentice House, 2008). Other stories I was working on included "Out for a Walk," published by *The Baltimore Review* in 2007, and "Cicadas."

I was inspired to write "Cicadas" in 2004, when the landscape in Baltimore was entirely transformed by the sound, look, smell, and feel of Brood X. It was like nothing I had experienced before.

When East Baltimore's Patterson Theater hosted a reading of *Write Here Write Now* highlights in 2006, "Cicadas" became the first short story I read aloud to an audience as an author outside an academic setting. "Cicadas" would go on to be read on Baltimore's NPR station, WYPR, in 2008, and published as the opening story in *New Lines from the Old Line State: An Anthology of Maryland Writers* (Maryland Writers Association Press, 2008).

Fast forward a decade to 2018. I decided to challenge myself by registering for a three-day novel contest. I scanned my file cabinet drawer of one-page story treatments and decided to tackle one with the working title *Divorce Courting*.

Sometimes when developing characters for a novel or story, I review characters from past works to see if anyone fits the role and timeframe.

As I started to flesh out some of the scenes and ideas for the new novel, I began to see that the narrator of "Cicadas" was a suitable fit for *Divorce Courting*. Then the thought emerged like a swarm of insects: the cicadas were returning in 2021—just a few years away at the time.

In "Cicadas," Stu considers where he was the last time the cicadas emerged in 1987, and contemplates where he will be the next time they wake in 2021. The perpetual bachelor, seeing his friends married, begins to wonder whether he's wrong in his comparisons of love and buzzing insect hoards.

Thus, *Wrecks and Ruins* became more than the off-again, on-again romantic comedy originally anticipated—it became an exploration of a young man turned middle-aged and what had changed and remained the same from one cicada cycle to the next. I think of *Wrecks and Ruins* as a "coming of (a certain) age story."

In the original story from 2006 that follows, you'll note echoes and passages that carry over to *Wrecks and Ruins*. These are intentional.

Will Stu still be around and worthy of a literary visit when the Cicadas return in 2038? Only time will tell.

— Eric D. Goodman
Baltimore, Maryland, 2021

# CICADAS

So, he was going to do it. *They* were going to do it. A few months of bliss together and they were ready to devote themselves entirely to one another forever. They had no idea what was coming.

I returned to northern Virginia that year, the year the cicadas returned. It was the summer of 2004, and my friend Skip was tying the knot. Leona was the most wonderful woman he had ever gotten to know. They were intimate, in love, soul mates. So alike, they looked and acted like twin copies of the same person, male and female.

So I returned to Virginia for their wedding—one I never expected to see, Skip not seeming the marrying type. I arrived a day early for the rehearsal. I drove into the wooded hills, my windows rolled down to enjoy the warm summer air cooled only by my speed. The uncanny noise started soft and dull, nearly unnoticeable. But it grew louder and fuller, an incessant screeching.

By the time I'd reached my destination it was unearthly, a crescendo from nature, unnatural. It was an eerie alien landscape, a scene from an old 1950s bug-eyed monster movie with sound effects so bizarre they couldn't possibly be real. But this sound *was* real. It was nearly off-putting enough to make me turn around and return to the comfort of my home, where I'd postponed a romantic rendezvous of my own.

Skip and Leona had heard whispers. Older friends and relatives, those experienced in life, had warned them that the cicadas were coming this year. But that didn't deter them. An outdoor wedding was what they wanted and an outdoor wedding was what they would have.

Looking at them in the park under the warmth of the afternoon sun and the spell of love, it seemed they were younger than they had been. Skip was more naïve now, the day before his wedding, than he had been years ago when we were still in high school, back when he was devising the best strategy for asking a girl to the prom without risking rejection. When he found a taker after two strikes, he was convinced he was in love. That affair had lasted five weeks and ended in emotional disaster.

But this one had already endured more than three months. They were so in love that they barely noticed the strange insects all around them, Skip in his tee-shirt with the imprint of a tux, and she in her matching wedding tee. But they were too inexperienced to understand such a commitment, unaware of the cycle. They didn't remember the last time the cicadas had come.

Clint sat at one of the aluminum picnic benches under the pavilion, drinking a beer. As one of the groomsmen, he was wearing his tux. He'd forgotten this was an informal rehearsal. He slammed his fist against the table, the momentary look of anger on his face lifting as he flung something from his hand and then wiped away the remains. He stood and walked toward the trash barrel, then saw me approaching. He glanced back toward Skip and his bride to be. "Stu's here."

The cicadas had come seventeen years ago as well. And at that time, too, I was arriving in northern Virginia—that time, for the first time, to live. Halfway through high school, in 1987, I came to the school that would send me out into the world.

I met Skip and Clint that year, the year of the cicadas. It was during that year, shortly after I came to know him, that Clint married his own first true love, Amanda. His was an indoor wedding—Clint was no fan of insects—though the buzzing of the cicadas could be heard through the manmade boundaries of the divine structure. Clint had dropped out of high school with only a year left so he could do the honorable thing, the thing that he wanted to do not just because he had gotten Amanda pregnant but because he loved her. I envied him at the time and wished I could be so bold, parting with convention and leaving the tortures of public school to get a beautiful girl pregnant and marry her.

I had a run at it. It was during those noisy days of cicada love songs that I found my own first true love—a love that ended as the cicadas were dying off at the summer's end. I courted her alongside the cicadas, serenaded her with their voices instead of my own, and mated with her alongside them during camping trips. Before their eggs were falling from tree branches and delivering offspring to burrow into the earth for another seventeen years, our own relationship had dried up, crushed like the insect husks covering the sidewalks.

I learned a lot about love that summer. Clint did, too. So did Skip.

Now, at the wedding rehearsal, the groom gave me an emotional hug and Leona gave me an obligatory one. "You had us a little worried there for a minute," Skip said.

"Am I ever late?" I asked.

Clint scoffed. "But are you ever early?" His handshake pulled me into a bear hug.

"Let's get going," Skip said, anxious for the rehearsal, excited to get to tomorrow's real thing.

What Skip and Leona still didn't know—not yet—was what I didn't know the last time the cicadas had emerged: that romance is like the cycle of a cicada. There are a few weeks, perhaps a couple of months, of excited buzz—liveliness, romance, excitement, attraction, mating—and then comes a seventeen-year sleep; a lapse into monotony and routine that can't live up to the promise of the noisy romance at the start.

# 2

A lot had changed since high school, but the fact that we were friends had not. We all lived in different places—me north, Clint west, and Skip in Virginia—but we had managed to keep our friendship. A few times every year we met up in one place or another: sometimes a weekend at one of our houses, other times at a cabin in the woods or mountains or just a hotel room with a couple of beds and a sleeper sofa.

The last time we got together, Skip had arranged the gathering. A cabin in the Smokies for three days provided just the isolation Skip desired to break the news.

We spent our days hiking and our nights playing cards. We liked to do things like that, things that involved activity but no intense concentration. We played hearts and spades and seven-up. An occasional hand of poker, the winner with the most chips— potato chips, pretzels, or tortillas—chose who went on the next beer run.

"Remember back in high school?" Clint said as he finished dealing and picked up his hand, spreading it into a fan and ordering his cards. "We used to play every day." Skip and I smiled and nodded. We had this conversation most times we played cards, every three to four months. "Those were the days," Clint said, taking a swig of beer from a longneck and discarding the bottle.

We'd spent many a lunch break playing cards back in high school. We'd eat our cafeteria lunches, then clear our trays and pull out the deck. As adults, Clint never let us forget it. He had an excited memory of his youth, in part because it was lost prematurely in the webbing of his complicated marriage. When loosened by whiskey he sometimes admitted regrets: that he wished he'd finished high school and gone to college and not gotten married so young. He'd had a good shot at a football scholarship. He could have been a success, something he didn't feel he was to his own wife and three kids. "Yes, those were the days," he sighed.

Playing cards was one of our favorite things to do because it gave us an excuse to talk. Cards, hiking, fishing, eating, drinking—they were all excuses that allowed us to talk without admitting that talking was what we wanted to do. We couldn't talk about serious things without pretending the talk was a by-product of partaking in some other action. Playing cards was a husk.

By the time Skip won the next hand, we were out of beer. Clint threw his cards down. "Get the hell out!" he yelled angrily, thrashing his strong arm violently through the air in pursuit of a fly that had been buzzing around our table.

"*You* get the hell out!" Skip said, then grinned. "And get us some more beer."

Clint glared at him with mock irritation. "I'm going. You sissies practice so you'll be ready when I get back and really start playing." We laughed as he picked up his keys and left the cabin. Skip collected the cards.

"Hey, Stu." Skip looked at me with eyes that wanted to tell me something big, something monumental. *Probably something stupid*, I figured, but in his mind this was pivotal. Each eye twinkled on an axis of destiny. "I have something to ask you."

I looked at him with leery anticipation. *What's he want now? Help with his resume? A reference? A loan to start another business?* Most of the business plans he or I had been involved with were crushed dead at our feet within months of energized excitement. *Maybe love advice?* That's what it looked like, seeping from him. I'd had enough lovers to offer plenty of that. His eyes asked permission. "So ask," I said.

"Will you be my best man?"

I laughed. He was a boy catching his first insect of the season, offering her a comfortable place inside a glass jar, cushioned with dry grass, knife-jabbed holes in the metal lid and a stick inside for comfort. But Skip was offering this new lover more than the comfort of a stick; he offered her his freedom, his very life. He wanted to protect her within his glass jar and he wanted to be protected within hers.

"Seriously, man," he said. He tried not to show he was hurt by my dismissive laugh.

"You don't want to get married," I advised without seeking permission from his eyes. "That's crazy."

"I love Leona," he insisted. "Of course I want to marry her."

"I love women, too," I rebutted. "But you don't see me dragging any of them to the altar."

"You just haven't found the right one."

I laughed again, this time a little harder. "If there was a right one I've certainly had her." There had been quite a few right ones, which was exactly why I wasn't stupid enough to commit.

"So, what's it gonna be?" he asked. He had opened his protective layer of bark and I'd jabbed him. Now he was putting up the tough front. "Are you gonna be my best man or what?"

I considered. "If I'm the best man you can find." This pleased him. I was happy to be my friend's best man. I just wished I could convince him that this whole marriage thing wasn't the best idea.

Or maybe it was, for him. I suppose there's something to be said for the soul mate, whether self-created or truly destined. Maybe Skip could dig the comfort of having someone to burrow through the years with in the same way I could dig picking up anyone who put off the right pheromones at the right time without feeling the heavy weight of a marriage contract. But the feeling that Skip wasn't making the right decision, that Clint hadn't made the right decision seventeen years ago, echoed in my head.

If it was a soul mate or life partner Skip was looking for, Leona was probably the right one. But didn't he realize that their love was temporary and that in a month or two their buzzing romance would lie dead at their feet? The remains would burrow underground and remain dormant for years. And the two of them would be much happier and more alive if they shed the exoskeleton of their relationship when the newness ended and pursued happiness with fresh mates.

# 3

We were never the rowdiest bunch on the block. Skip, Clint and I had our fun, but it usually consisted of eating and drinking, going for a nature walk or catching a movie, playing cards and talking. We talked about movies we'd seen or books we'd read, if not recently, then back in high school. And we talked about our lives, at the moment, in the past and in the future. Our fun no longer included challenging each other with corny pick-up lines to use on women at singles bars. That had subdued when Clint married Amanda, and it ended entirely when Skip announced his engagement.

For Skip's bachelor's party we rented a hotel suite with a pool-side patio and went crazy with drinks, conversation, music and cards. Our friend, Dana, was a professional dee-jay and provided us with music of yesteryear and today.

It was three weeks until the big day, and the cicadas were out in full force, even at night. Dana had recorded them at ninety decibels earlier in the day. That's about how many lovers I'd enjoyed since the last time the cicadas came. But this night, the dancing girls we'd hired for the party left after only an hour—and spent only the last twenty minutes of it unclothed—so it looked liked the after-party would not be one of amorous love. Brotherly love would have to do.

The party ended around two in the morning as our scattered collection of friends and acquaintances left Skip, Clint and me alone. It was like one of our regular weekend getaways. Only a few weeks after this one, Skip was inheriting a potential pest.

Clint swatted at the cicadas. "Six weeks of this bullshit?" He swore at them, was angered by them.

"Leave the poor things alone," I said.

"These poor things are all going to be dead in a month anyway," he said.

Clint had become my opposite in many ways. In high school we had been alike; over the years that distanced us with space and time we had become counter to one another. For every movie he purchased, I bought a hardcover novel. For every healthy meal I ordered, he super-sized it. For every woman contenting me, he lingered on his discontent with Amanda. For each cicada he killed, I transplanted one from harm's way.

"Movie or a card game?" Skip asked.

"How about a quick game and then a movie?" Clint suggested.

"Fine." I sat at the outside table overlooking the moonlit swimming pool. Clint shuffled, I cut.

"Here, you deal." He handed the deck to Skip. With his hands free, Clint swatted at the cicadas. "Can't you damn bugs shut up?"

A half-bottle of Southern Comfort and five cans of beer remained. I poured us each a shot. "To women," I said. Clint chuckled humorlessly.

"No," Skip amended as he raised his glass. "To true love."

"Gimme a break," Clint said. We shot back the sweet drinks.

Skip finished his shot, but he wasn't finished on the subject. "Since meeting Leona, I've learned what true love is." We fanned our cards as Skip enlightened us. "True love is when you love someone so much that you don't need them as much as you need them to need you."

Clint spit out a sunflower seed. "True love is a crock of shit. I learned that the hard way." He laid down a heart. "By getting married." He jabbed Skip in the side playfully and then took a swig of beer.

"Don't you love Amanda?" Skip asked. "I mean, you bitch a lot about her, but you love her. She was one of the hottest girls in high school. You're lucky!"

"Lucky?" He considered. "Yes, I love her. But it's a different kind of love. It's... I don't know. Just be sure you know what you're doing, Skip. Know for sure she's the right one, that this is the right time." A hum filled the air when our conversation hit a pause.

I snapped a club into the center of the table. "Love's a cicada cycle."

"Oh, that's deep," Skip said with a windy sound that conveyed annoyance above amusement.

"No, really. The high of romance, then years and years of mundane routine. That's why I'm single."

"So you think it's better to never have it than to have it and lose it?"

"No," I said. "I get the exciting part. But when the excitement fades, detach. Find someone else and the buzz begins again. Single life offers all the buzz without the mess."

Clint came to his lifestyle's defense. "There's a lot to be said for family life, though. I love my kids more than you can imagine, Stu. I'm not saying it's the most exciting life, and sometimes I want to break out and be a kid again. But I wouldn't trade my family for the world." He took a drink of his beer and crushed the empty can. "I love them too much. It's not the exciting love of a first date. But it's a stronger bond than a single person could understand." He threw the can toward the trash.

"See?" Skip said. "The truth comes out. The glory days are fun to reminisce over, but they weren't really better. Love is better."

"Hey, I dig love," I said. "But give me budding romance and keep the ho-hum love of wilted flowers."

Skip put down his spades and won the game. "How about that movie?" He changed the subject from love to its opposite. "*Saving Private Ryan* or *Apocalypse Now*?"

"This is a bachelor party," I said. "It can't be a war movie. We need a sex comedy."

"Yes it can," Skip argued. "I'm blowing away my loneliness."

"Yuck," Clint reacted to the phrase. "*Apocalypse Now*."

"No," I disagreed. "*Saving Private Ryan*."

"*Full Metal Jacket* it is, then." Skip said.

The soundtrack of the war movie did battle with the cicadas outside, and their combination brought a thought: *Not just love, but war.*

Wars followed the cicada cycle: a nervous excitement, guns, tanks, testosterone, bombs and missiles, and then, after the hideous noise…silence. The cicadas ceased, like so many fallen soldiers on the shores of Normandy, in the sands of the Middle East and on the wrong side of the demilitarization zone. Now, as we watched our movie, our country was at war with Iraq, still lingering in Afghanistan, and fighting that elusive enemy known as terrorism. Two cicada cycles before, we were fighting in Vietnam. The last time the cicadas had come, we saw only minor conflicts in the Persian Gulf. Sometimes these things skipped a generation.

Like love and war, death also followed the cycle of the cicada. During the last cycle, my grandfather died. During this one, an uncle passed away. Whose soul would they sing for the next time around? My father's? My own?

# 4

Clint is an especially forceful nose-blower. He's been known to blow holes in tissue paper. It's usually best if he does his business behind the closed door of a stall, behind the second closed door of a bathroom. But he never does, of course. Clint likes to make a show of things, likes to display his force, his dirty mucus, his mundane life, his miserable marriage, his poor parenting and his misbehaving kids. *Clint's example helped form my own list of things to avoid,* I realized for the first time at Skip's wedding. It wasn't coincidence that we'd become opposites, pawns at the far ends of a chess board. I like to keep my affairs secret; I blow my nose in private, and increasingly so as old age brings about stronger and more defined allergies. Allergies are just one of the weaknesses that come with age, position and place. It's only one of the insecurities of security.

There must have been three hundred guests at the wedding, not including the cicadas. Clint and Amanda were there, but Clint was more focused on the other women in attendance. Amanda noticed it more with acknowledgement than anger. He looked, but he didn't touch. *It's okay to imagine strangling your kids, as long as you don't really do it,* Amanda had once said. She knew her husband was true to her and loyal to their family.

By now Clint had expanded his arsenal. His hand was no longer enough to combat the annoying foe. Decked out in his tux and tails, he carried a black fly-swatter with him and used it violently.

There were others present that I knew but didn't know. People I remembered from high school, but didn't really remember. Faces familiar but without names. Names that, when introduced, I'd heard before but didn't remember, or remembered incorrectly, faces and names skewed, not matching my memory of them. The Rubik's Cube I never quite had the patience to solve beyond one side, phantoms from yearbooks, manifested but deformed.

It was a nice service, a beautiful wedding. The shade trees stood alive with the cicada noises we had all become accustomed to. The screeching radiated from the branches, providing an applause so loud that it competed even with

Dana's music at the outdoor reception that followed in the same location.

I could barely hear the song end beneath the drone of the insects; that was my cue. I tapped my knife against my glass and stood. "Ladies and gentlemen, friends, family and guests." All eyes came my way. "Now's the part where I say something nice for the lovely couple." I looked at Skip and Leona. They looked lovelier than the newlyweds on the top of their cake, happier than a pair of cicadas newly emerged from the earth. "We have a lot of guests here from all over the country. But if you listen, you'll hear that there are quite a few uninvited guests, too." I paused to let the song of the cicadas illustrate the point.

Skip and Leona looked concerned that I might ruin their day.

"Seventeen years ago I came to Virginia for the first time—that's when I met Skip—and we've been the best of friends ever since. Now, with the return of the cicadas, I've returned to Virginia to visit Skip and share in his celebration of love with Leona." I strained to say the thing that I knew I needed to say. I strained to mean it, to believe it could be so for someone, if not for me. I looked directly at the happy Skip and Leona. "I hope that seventeen years from now, when the cicadas sing their love songs again, I have the chance to return and visit the two of you, still happy, still together, and still in love."

It was a decent toast; at least the audience seemed to like it as they all raised their glasses with me in honor of the newlyweds. But as I finished my Champagne and returned to my seat, as the music resumed with a soft tune and Skip and Leona took to the floor and initiated the dancing, as I listened to the cicadas sing their own song, I wondered. Skip and Leona would have a delightful few weeks. But then, when the romance faded into mundane affection, and then into dormant co-existence, would they remain happy? When the cicadas stopped their buzz and fell dead, would their love do the same? Would Skip and Leona survive the silence?

After a bit of dancing, Skip and Leona approached me. "You had us a little worried for a minute," Skip said, gleaming.

I laughed. "Have I ever shamed you in public?"

Skip smiled. "I won't answer that now. This is a happy occasion."

Clint and Amanda joined in. "It'll get even better," Amanda said. "It changes, romantic love. It gets deeper, more meaningful."

"Now we just have to do something about Stu," Clint said.

"Me? I can take care of myself." There were plenty of girls at the wedding to choose from, and more back home—some yet unmet.

"Sure," Leona said. "But there's someone out there who can take care of you better than you can. It's just a matter of time."

"Right." Amanda smiled. "After all, Stu, you can't live like that forever."

# 5

The day after the wedding, the happy couple flew south for their honeymoon and it was time for us—the guests—to scatter. I drove north.

The cicadas were dying already. The sound was still there, but it wasn't as loud as it had been. It didn't take long for me to exhaust my supply of windshield fluid; cicada splatters decorated my windshield. A few even entered my car, one of them smacking me in the face with more force than I would have expected from such a small creature.

The lush, green trees surrounding the road were freckled with brown spots where the moisture of life had been sucked dry by the hungry insects. The trees stood tall and proud, but blemished, diseased, broken down by too much excitement. Huge blotches of leaves were left dry and without purpose, except that of drifting groundward to decay. Much as my life had been sucked dry by my playboy ways and left meaningless except for the excitement I allowed to feed upon me as I fed upon it.

Part of me wanted to join the cicadas in the earth, to sample the quite life of mundane normalcy. To slow down and not be in such a hurry for the next squeeze, the next thrill. To join Skip and Clint in the good life. Was I going nowhere fast, fleeing the inevitable green lawn and white, picket fence? But as roadside trees gave way to concrete and buildings—as I came closer to my apartment in the city—I stomped out the thought as best I could. Better wait and see how the good life held up for my friends.

We would see one another in a few months. We would see how Skip was feeling then. The cicadas would be dead by then. They were dying already.

# ABOUT THE AUTHOR

Eric D. Goodman writes in Maryland, where he lives with his wife of twenty-eight years, two children, and English Springer Spaniel. He is author of *The Color of Jadeite* (Loyola University's Apprentice House Press, 2020), *Setting the Family Free* (Apprentice House Press, 2019), *Womb: a novel in utero* (Merge Publishing, 2017) *Tracks: A Novel in Stories* (Atticus Books, 2011), and *Flightless Goose*, (Writers Lair Press, 2008). More than a hundred short stories, articles, and travel stories have been published in literary journals and magazines. Learn more about Eric and his writing at www.EricDGoodman.com or connect with him at www.Facebook.com/EricDGoodman.

Apprentice
House Press
*Loyola University Maryland*

Apprentice House is the country's only campus-based, student-staffed book publishing company. Directed by professors and industry professionals, it is a nonprofit activity of the Communication Department at Loyola University Maryland.

Using state-of-the-art technology and an experiential learning model of education, Apprentice House publishes books in untraditional ways. This dual responsibility as publishers and educators creates an unprecedented collaborative environment among faculty and students, while teaching tomorrow's editors, designers, and marketers.

Outside of class, progress on book projects is carried forth by the AH Book Publishing Club, a co-curricular campus organization supported by Loyola University Maryland's Office of Student Activities.

Eclectic and provocative, Apprentice House titles intend to entertain as well as spark dialogue on a variety of topics. Financial contributions to sustain the press's work are welcomed. Contributions are tax deductible to the fullest extent allowed by the IRS.

To learn more about Apprentice House books or to obtain submission guidelines, please visit www.apprenticehouse.com.

Apprentice House
Communication Department
Loyola University Maryland
4501 N. Charles Street
Baltimore, MD 21210
410-617-5265
info@apprenticehouse.com • www.apprenticehouse.com

CPSIA information can be obtained
at www.ICGtesting.com
Printed in the USA
FSHW011605291221
87157FS

9 781627 203845